D0921729

Sheisty
Triple Crown Collection

Sheisty
Triple Crown Collection

T.N. Baker

www.urbanbooks.net

Urban Books, LLC
97 N18th Street
Wyandanch, NY 11798

Sheisty: Triple Crown Collection

ISBN 13: 978-1-62286-928-2
ISBN 10: 1-62286-928-1

Reprint Trade Paperback Publication April 2015
Printed in the United States of America

10 9 8 7 6 5 4 3 2 1

Distributed by Kensington Publishing Corp.
Submit Orders to:
Customer Service
400 Hahn Road
Westminster, MD 21157-4627
Phone: 1-800-733-3000
Fax: 1-800-659-2436

DEDICATION

Tiana, my star, Mommy loves you.

ACKNOWLEDGMENTS

I have to thank God first for giving me the ability to write. It's because of Him that I have the strength to continue, survive, and face my everyday struggles. Everybody has a story to tell, but not everybody can write about it. So, God, I thank you for the gift of being able to write about my thoughts as well as my experiences.

Chloe A. Hilliard, not only do I love having you as my editor, but I also want to thank you for being more than just that. Thank you for going the extra mile. Your encouraging words and support have meant so much to me, and for that I greatly appreciate you.

Mother, I think half of *Sheisty's* sales came from you. I know you're proud of me. Thanks for your support, I love you!

Daddy, I know you're watching over me with a smile. Nothing compares to you. I'll always love you and miss your presence.

To my beautiful daughter, Tiana: you are truly the love of my life. I can't imagine my life without you.

Grandma, thanks for always being there for me. I love you with all my heart.

To the best sisters in the world: Tana, Tanean, and Vicki. I know I might not always show it or say it much, but I love the shit out of y'all.

My nieces, Zhana and Nehemyah Nicole, and nephews, Isaiah and Mica, Auntie loves you guys!

Acknowledgments

My gorgeous god daughter Badriyah, I love you.

To my brother-in-law, Michael, my aunts and uncles (especially you, Uncle Andre, for all that you did for me as a kid, and just for being a cool-ass uncle since you got older): I love you! Oh yeah, Auntie Barbara, I know you gon' make sure all your coworkers and internet buddies purchase my books. Luv ya!

To all my cousins: I love you guys.

My best friend, Aisha, I'm glad you're back in N.Y., girl. I miss hanging out with you!

Wa boogie, thanks for putting me up on the first book to ever spark my interest (*The Coldest Winter Ever*). I've been hooked on reading ever since. I hope you can find it in your heart to be my friend again. I love and miss you!

To my TCP family: much love. Keep dropping the hot books!

Vickie Stringer, thanks for believing in me, putting me down with your crown, and pushing my book the way you do. Much love!

Last but not least, to all my fans that supported *Sheisty*, *Still Sheisty*, and *Sheisty Revised*, I thank you from the bottom of my heart.

EPIPHANY

I didn't know who sang the old school song, but I turned up the radio volume and sang the hook as loud as I could. "Use what you got to get what you want." Ain't that the truth.

I was twenty-two years old, pushing a 325 BMW, living in a $700 a month apartment, all being funded by the power of the pussy. Shit, with beauty and a booty, who needed a job? I mean, let's not get it twisted. I wasn't no dummy. I did graduate from high school. I even thought about college briefly when Keisha went. Then I remembered how glad I was to finally be finished with high school. Me, with a job? Never! For one, I didn't like being told what to do. I hated getting up in the morning, and being on time was just something I wasn't good at.

Now sex—I could do that. And for money, I could do it all day. Don't get me wrong; I wasn't no street-corner ho or nothing like that. I just preferred to date guys with money that didn't mind paying to play, because after a good time, the bills still had to get paid.

It's like my mother always said: "If you want quality, you gotta pay for it," and Epiphany Janee Wright is top of the line quality.

I was excited about my date that night with Smitty, a potential "sponsor." Sponsor, buyer, or trick were just some of the little titles me and my girls liked to use to describe these niggas out here tricking, a.k.a. financially taking care of a woman's needs.

I met him at the club the night before, and from the looks of it, he had a lot of cash. But what impressed me was the bottle of Dom P he sent over to my table, along with his number. Now, that's class. Most guys will press hard for the digits but won't come up outta them pockets to buy a drink. Hmm, first impressions are the best impressions.

I glanced at the clock. It was 6:00 p.m. Smitty was picking me up in two hours, and knowing me, it was gonna take every bit of that two hours to get ready.

I hopped in the shower and was dressed, looking and smelling good, at exactly 8:00 p.m. I was so excited about possibly gaining a new sponsor that I forgot to call Malikai, my current trick, with an excuse for why I wouldn't be seeing him that night. I was surprised that I hadn't heard from him all day. There was no question about it: his ass was sprung, and I wanted to keep it that way. Whatever it took to keep his cash flowing my way, I'd do. I wasn't tryin'a mess that up, and the key was just keeping the nigga happy. Any real woman knows how to keep a man happy. You just fuck 'em when they wanna be fucked and tell 'em what they wanna hear.

Smitty showed up an hour late, blowing the horn of his Expedition truck like I was the one that kept him waiting. When I got in the truck, I could tell he was still pleased with my looks by the smile on his face. On the other hand, he didn't look as good as I thought—which was a slight disappointment—but he appeared to be paid, and that's what's up. Money does make a difference. I've seen it turn a frog into prince and a beast into a beauty queen on many occasions, especially in the entertainment industry. I won't name no names. They know who they are.

"So, where we going?" I asked.

"Yo, I gotta make a stop at my crib first and then we'll go get something to eat, a'ight?" he said.

I sucked my teeth and rolled my eyes at him as I thought, *I let him slide for being late, but now he's pushing it.*

Smitty had this cockiness about him. I wasn't feeling his personality at all, and my attitude was starting to show it. To top it off, he lived with his mother in the projects. Don't get me wrong, I don't have nothing against a nigga from the projects getting paper, but if you could splurge out thirty G's or more for a truck, your next move should be to come up outta the PJs.

"Yo, come on 'cause I'ma be a minute, and I ain't trying to leave your fine-ass out here around these niggas," Smitty said.

I wasn't sure if he meant they would be trying to push up on me or rob me, so I went with him into the three-story building. Upstairs, the apartment was a mess. His mother looked like she was his number one customer, assuming he had to be a drug dealer. I followed him to the back of the three-bedroom apartment, to a steel door with four locks on it.

When Smitty opened the door to his room, to my surprise, it didn't even look like a part of the dingy apartment. He had a nice bedroom set, stereo equipment, a DVD player, and all the CDs and DVD movies you could possibly think of. His shit was laced. Nevertheless, I wasn't impressed. It was still just a room at his mom's in the projects.

He locked the door, turned on his stereo, blasting Black Rob's "Like Whoa," and put a movie on also and muted the sound. Then he opened up a safe down by the side of the bed. It was filled with drugs, money, two guns, and some jewelry. He lifted his pant leg, pulled a stack of money tied in a rubber band out of his sock, counted it, and placed it in the safe.

As he shut the door to the safe, he quickly glanced over at me to see if I was looking. I pretended to be glued to the television.

Smitty came over to me and started to caress my leg, talking loudly over the music about how good I looked and how badly he wanted to fuck me. I laughed, because I found this nigga hilarious. Here it is, he hadn't even spend any real money yet and already he was pushing up on the pussy.

"Nigga, please. Look, you got shit twisted, Smitty. I don't know what you are used to, but this ass right here ain't free." I got straight to the point, since I already knew I wasn't gon' fuck with his ugly frontin'-like-he-stacking, still-livin'-with-his-momma-ass.

The look on his face turned cold. What was I thinking? As a matter of fact, I wasn't thinking. I was locked in a room with this thug-ass nigga, and no one knew where I was or who I was with. No sooner than that thought crossed my mind, Smitty grabbed me by my throat and forcefully got on top off me.

"Bitch, do you know who the fuck I am? I ain't never had to pay fo' no pussy, and I ain't 'bout to start."

I felt helpless and almost breathless from the tight grip he had on my neck. Tears streamed down the sides of my face as he pulled my panties to the side with his free hand and rammed his dick inside me. It seemed like forever, although it was only a few strokes long. I couldn't believe that I was being violated like this, and all I could think about was what he might do next.

Suddenly, he pulled his dick out, bust his nut all over me and arrogantly said, "I took the pussy, you trick-ass bitch. Now what? Just fix your shit and get the fuck out!"

KEISHA

Tucker was really starting to get on my nerves. It had to be my hormones tripping me out, because I loved the ground he walked on, but sometimes his excitement of having his first-born drove me nuts.

These last few months had been moving so slowly. I barely saw my friends anymore. Once in a while, Shana would call or stop by with gifts for the baby and small talk, but Epiphany had become so distant. I'd called and left several messages on her machine. I even asked Malikai to tell her to call me. To be honest, I didn't know what was up with her. She acted like pregnancy was contagious. Tucker and I had been engaged for over a month and I hadn't even been able to share the news with her. It hurt to feel like I was losing not only my best friend, but more like my sister.

Shit, I felt closer to her and her family than I did my own blood. Epiphany and I grew up together. I always admired the fact that she was raised in such a loving household by her mother and her father. Me, on the other hand, I was just the opposite. I don't even remember my father, and my mother being an alcoholic was all I seemed to remember.

I spent a lot of nights over Epiphany's house to get away from my mother. E's parents always treated me like family. Sometimes that girl didn't realize how lucky she was to have concerned parents that gave her the world.

Besides Epiphany, Tucker was the only other person I considered to be family. I had two younger sisters that lived in Atlanta with our grandmother, who always had her hand out for something. She thought since Tucker was high-rolling, it was our responsibility to help her support my sisters. And speaking of support, I hadn't heard from my so-called mother, Loretta, since I moved in with Tucker five years ago.

My childhood had made me a little bitter, but at the same time, I learned from it. I always felt as if I was ahead of my class. So, to get out faster, I dropped out of high school in the eleventh grade, got my G.E.D., and completed four years of college a year ahead of time. I was going back for my master's after my baby was born.

So you see, I did have a plan. I was not about to let life pass me by, while I sat around feeling sorry for myself like my mother did. I would give my child the life I never had, no matter what it took.

I'd been with Tucker since I was sixteen. He was the only man I'd ever been with sexually. I loved him dearly. If something were to happen to him, I didn't think that I would make it. That was why I wished he would leave the drug game alone.

Tucker made a lot of money selling dope. Business for him was always good, so the money was definitely consistent, and you know what that means: more money, more problems. I knew he loved me, so I didn't worry about losing him to another woman, but the streets? Now, that was a different story.

SHANA

It was Friday, and all I could think about was hitting the club that night. Since K.C., my abusive-ass man, got locked up two days before, I didn't have to worry about him running up on me in the clubs no more, trying to smack a bitch up 'cause I was out doing the same shit he was doing. K.C. was my nigga, no doubt, and he had some good dick, but he thought just because he spent his money on me, he owned my ass.

I remember one time, me and Epiphany was hanging out at Cheetah's on a Friday night, having the time of our life, when here this nigga comes up from out of nowhere, making a scene, talking 'bout, "Go home."

I'm like, "What! Go home?" Yo, the way that nigga was acting threw me way off, 'cause I just started fucking around with him.

Right then and there I should've seen the "beat a bitch" signs written all over his ass, but you know how that goes. Instead, I just thought the nigga was really feeling me like that, 'cause I'm thinking, *Why else would he lose it and wanna beat the shit out of me if he ain't care?*

Most of the time it was my fault anyway. I was just the type of chick that was gonna do what the fuck I wanted to do and deal with the consequences later. Needless to say, getting my ass kicked was always the consequences for fucking with his ass. We stayed on some war of the roses type of shit, 'cause he wasn't gon' just be fucking me up without getting a few bumps and bruises too. I'll go hard for mines. But that was still my boo, and shit, y'all know what they say: Love is blinder than a muthafucka.

Epiphany couldn't stand K.C. One time she went as far as to say he tried to holla at her. Now, don't get me wrong; that was my homegirl. I'd known her for years, but most of the time I just wasn't feeling her whole attitude. She thought every nigga wanted to get with her.

When she told me that, I couldn't say the thought of it maybe being true didn't bother me, but he denied it, and I believed him. Shit, this nigga was taking care of me, and I loved how he took care of me. On top of that, did I mention the sex was the *bomb*?

I wasn't letting shit come in between us for nobody—until this nigga went and did some dumb shit and got locked the fuck up for a third felony charge. Three strikes and you're out, so there wasn't no need in trying to hold on, 'cause K.C. was finished, finito, outta here. He was locked up for the rest of his life. Shit, I wasn't that stand-by-your-man type of bitch—not if the nigga was doing a lifelong bid. I'll tell you this much though: that was a waste of some good dick, and I would damn sure miss his ass.

My skills weren't as tight as Epiphany's when it came to pulling a nigga that would spend his dough on me, so when I pulled K.C., I tried to hold onto his ass.

Epiphany had it good, 'cause she grew up in a house. It didn't matter what the neighborhood was like, as long as it was a house. With niggas, that played a big part in the amount of respect they gave you. On top of that, she was a pretty girl, plus all-the-way high maintenance. So, a nigga knew if he came at her, he had to come correct.

Me, I was a cutie, but I was from the PJs, so with that fact alone, it didn't matter what I looked like. Right off the back, niggas didn't respect me. They stereotyped me hard, assuming I was a ho or I had three or four kids by different daddies.

One thing that did make me better than Epiphany, though, was that I could rock with a dude for his cash, but I also knew how to get out there and get my own paper. I was a hustler, any way it came—boosting, credit card scams, cell phone hookups, or transporting shit out of town for the cats around my way. You named it, along with the right price, and I was down. Natural born hustler was in my blood, so with or without a trick-ass nigga, I was gonna get mine regardless, 'cause I loved the dough.

I had just started dancing at this strip club called Honey's. Yo! I made $500 in three short hours just off pussy-popping to some R&B and Hip Hop. Now, that's what's up. Shit, for some people, that's a month's rent, some food in the fridge, with a little pocket change left over for the club.

I was thinking about putting Epiphany on, 'cause she'd make a killing, and for that kind of easy cash, her money-hungry-ass just might be down to do it. But knowing her, she'd only steal the spotlight and fuck up my shine, so on second thought, I'd keep my shit on the low.

EPIPHANY

Shana had been calling me all day. I knew she wanted to hit the club that night. Lately I hadn't been in the mood to do anything. It had been a week since that muthafucka got me for some pussy. All I knew was I got the hell outta there as fast as I could. Anyway, fuck that nigga. He got that—for now.

That wasn't the first time the pussy had been taken, though, and that whole situation just brought back memories. When I was a kid, my father's brother lived with us, and I remembered him always sweating me. He would always be like, "C'mere," bragging to his boys about my cuteness, saying, "Yo, I got a fly-ass little niece. She gon' put a hurting on them cats when she get older."

Uncle Ramel was always buying me gifts and giving me money. Then, at the tender age of twelve, he took my virginity—only he ain't grab me by my neck and force himself inside of me. It wasn't nothing like what that stupid muthafucka Smitty did to me. It was a gentle kind of rape. He was my uncle, my father's baby bro, and I trusted him.

It was uncomfortable at first, but shit, it went on for so long that I started to enjoy it. He was eighteen at the time and out there slanging them thangs for my father, so his gifts always got better, and so did the amounts of cash he would give me. By the time I was fifteen and he was twenty-one, I was fucking and sucking his dick like a *professional.* Call it sick, but after a while, you adjust to a situation. That is, until the nigga started getting jealous when boys came around, acting as if I was his girlfriend or something.

His behavior made me realize how sick he really was. I started to feel disgusting, him carrying on like that. I would fuck with him by putting emphasis on *Uncle* when I called him. Every time he would look at me and I felt it was inappropriate, I would always threaten to tell my father, just to have control over him.

Guess he couldn't take the heat anymore, or the chance that I might one day tell, so he moved out. Now we tried to avoid each other as much as possible, but when I did see him at family functions, I got off on flaunting my cuteness in his face and calling him *Uncle* Ramel. He still looked at me like he wanted me, but what could he say? He created a monster.

I guess that's where I got my "get what I can get with the pussy" attitude from, huh? Shit, everything came with a price. Thinking back on all this was crazy, but the point I'm trying to make is even my uncle paid for the pussy, and so would Smitty, one way or another!

I picked up Shana a little after midnight. In New York, the parties were just getting started around 1:00 a.m. It was the weekend, so I knew the traffic would be a little crazy once we hit the city. Shit, you had to fight with the yellow cabs just to get to your destination.

The club was off the hook, as usual—except I needed to party with the very important people. Since I had the gift of gab to go along with my beauty, I was always able to talk a man into anything. After downing a straight shot of Hennessey, I knew working my gift on the big, ugly bouncer, who was guarding the VIP section like it was a meal, would be a piece of cake.

B.I.G.'s "Big Poppa" was playing. Dom P, Cristal, and bottles of water were all the bar was selling. Now, for those (like me) who didn't know, the water was for the ecstasy poppers. Shana let me in on that secret, because she got down too.

"Girl, what don't your project-ass do?" I laughed. "Shit, I don't need a pill to enhance my sex. If a nigga's pockets is stacking and he don't mind splurging, then I'm like Burger King, he can have it his way."

There were definitely a few hit record makers in the house, along with a couple of one-hit wonders still trying to floss from a hit they made five to ten years ago. I mingled away from Shana because she was being a real groupie. I kept telling her these niggas didn't respect groupies. If you wanted them to notice you, you had to act as if you were just as important as they were and not pay they asses no mind (You know, a discreet groupie, like myself).

By the end of the night, the champagne had me feeling real horny, and since my discretion wasn't working, I called Malikai on his cell and told him to meet me at my place. He didn't ask any questions before he agreed, and why should he? It was five o' clock in the morning, and the only thing I knew that opened up at that time was legs. He knew exactly what I wanted—to be buck naked, getting fucked, listening to some R. Kelly's "Bump and Grind" until the smell of boodussy filled the air (meaning booty, dick, and pussy). When the smell of sweat and sex hit the air, you knew that shit was good.

Malikai had spent the past two nights with me. I could tell he wanted to take our relationship to another level. He was such a sweetie, and we did have a lot of fun together, but if his pockets didn't run deep, he might've been history a long time ago. We'd been kicking it for maybe about a year now, and his dick game had always been kinda whack, plus it was smaller than your average small penis.

I always wondered if a nigga with a little dick knew his shit was little. Somebody had to get pissed off or frustrated and tell his ass at some point in his life. It was always a catch-22 with these niggas. If he looked good, nine times out of ten the nigga was walking with deep pockets and a short reach (meaning he wasn't coming up off no dough). If he had some dough and freely gave it up, he was either ugly as hell, horrible in bed, or sometimes both.

Who knew if I'd ever settle down. Maybe one day I'd get lucky, maybe not, but if that was the case, I surely didn't have a problem with being single and having fun.

I guess everybody couldn't be lucky like Keisha, with a good-looking, faithful man who took care of her, stacked dough like crazy, and let her tell it, was a freak in bed too. Shit, fuck the best of both worlds; she had the whole world in her hands.

Speaking of Keisha, I had to call and see how she was doing. I couldn't believe she was gonna be a baby's momma. Better her than me. I was a strong believer when it came to abortion. Shit, I'd already had seven, please believe it. I didn't have no time to be having nobody's baby.

KEISHA

I got a call from Epiphany, and we actually made plans to check out a movie and grab a bite to eat that afternoon. I was upset with the way she'd been treating me since I got pregnant. Hanging out with Shana and E, reminiscing on old times, made it all better though. I laughed so much I almost peed in my pants three times. I hadn't seen Epiphany in about five months. To them, the past seven months went by fast; for me, it wasn't moving fast enough.

"I really miss you guys," I said, startin' to get teary-eyed. E laughed then reached over and gave me a tight hug, while Shana teased me for getting so emotional. I finally got to announce my engagement. Although Tucker and I hadn't set a date, I made both my girls promise to be there when we got married. We were having such a good time that I didn't want it to end.

So much was going on with them; it was hard playing catch up. Besides the baby and getting engaged, I didn't have anything to discuss that was as juicy as what was going on in their lives. All I knew was I couldn't wait to drop this load, not because I felt like I was missing out on what was in the streets, but because I was lonely and I missed times like these with my homegirls. For once, Epiphany didn't say anything to piss Shana off, which was good but rare.

Lately, Tucker had been back and forth out of town a lot. I was used to him being gone all the time, but he had promised to stay in town more toward the end of my pregnancy. His bullshit was really starting to bother me. Every time I said something, he said I was adding on to his stress, or I didn't have his back. So, I just keep quiet, but when his son got here, that nigga had better change his program.

I'd been spending a lot of time on the computer, meeting some interesting people online. I was logging into those kinky chat rooms, since I hadn't been getting much loving. What's wrong with living vicariously through others? Hell, I think I was addicted. I went by the name of BAPS, meaning bomb-ass pussy sweet. It was just innocent fun. Besides, it helped me keep my mind off my man's whereabouts.

SHANA

I was glad that Epiphany finally got around to hanging with Keisha. The girl got on my nerves asking about her all the time. She had to realize that we were all grown up now and shit wasn't gon' be like it used to. Everybody was livin' their own life. It was cool getting together and chillin' like back in the days, but this wasn't back in the day, and that close shit was slowly fading.

I met this chick, Chasity, from Pomanock Projects in Flushing. She got her dance on out in Jersey, too. We took the Path train together. She was cool as hell. I didn't fuck with too many bitches, but we just clicked. One night, we were doing a gig out in Brooklyn with this other chick she was cool with from out there. I didn't really want to fuck with Brooklyn 'cause that shit was just too close to home. I wasn't ready to be on front street shaking my ass, but fuck it—$150 for three sets plus tips wasn't bad at all.

When we arrived at the spot, it looked sort of like a warehouse inside, but it was set up real nice. I noticed there was nothing but girls up in there. Now, I know how chicks like to pile up in the club when it's free before ten o'clock, but it was almost twelve.

"Yo, I know we ain't dancing for no girls," I said to Chasity, who didn't seem surprised at all.

"I didn't wanna tell you 'cause I knew you wouldn't be with it, but dancing for the women is where them dollars is at, girl."

It didn't take much to convince me. I'd done worse shit than that. Hell, these chicks liked what the niggas like, so how bad could it be? She still could've told me though.

Chasity's homegirl's stage name was Scar. I asked her, "Why Scar?" She said it was 'cause if she didn't leave a scar on a nigga's heart, she'd damn sure leave one on his pockets. Now, that was deep. I thought to myself that her and Epiphany would probably get along good.

I decided to call myself Cream, so I chose "Ice Cream" by Wu Tang Clan as my introduction song.

I couldn't believe how wild they went when I came out on stage. Those dollars was flying. The shit was a rush for me, because women are your worse critics, but these chicks liked what they saw. I even got a few numbers handed to me after my dance, but I wasn't with that carpet munch shit.

EPIPHANY

Malikai was going out of town a lot more since his boy Tucker had to stay closer to home until his baby was born. Malikai was starting to bore me. He never wanted to do nothing but lay up when we were together. The money was still good, but he was out of town more than he was home. Shit, the nigga even had a crib down in North Carolina. He invited me to come chill with him, but I wasn't feeling him anymore, and the sooner he caught the hint the better.

It was comedy night at the Manhattan Proper. The spot was off the hook and always packed with niggas. A lot of Brooklyn cats were up in there too, I guess because they said Queens girls looked good. Should you expect anything less from a borough called Queens?

Shana's ass hadn't called me back yet, even after I paged her "911" about an hour before. Fuck her. It could've been important. She'd been on some different shit lately. I didn't know what, but I wasn't fucking with her.

I called up Tanya, this girl I went to high school with. We had run into each other about a week ago at the mall and exchanged numbers. She was cool enough to hang out with.

Tanya was with it and she could drive, so for once I didn't have to be the designated driver. She came to get me around 10:30 p.m. 'cause you gotta get there early if you want a good seat. We smoked a little weed to help us get silly, just in case the show wasn't funny.

It was exactly 10:45 when we arrived. The only seats that were available were by the bar, which was cool, but the people talking around the bar made it hard to hear the jokes.

I ordered a Henny on the rocks and an Amaretto Sour for Tanya, while she went to the restroom. That girl was crazy. You should never go to the bathroom while the comedians are performing, 'cause you have to pass the stage, and they will crack on your ass. She got off easy this time though, 'cause the girl that walked behind her was comical—wearing some shit she knew her big ass shouldn't have had on. Somebody should have warned her, because the comedian lit her ass up.

"Girl, some guy was trying to talk to me just now by the pay phones. He said he'll be over to buy us some drinks," Tanya said, all excited. I just smiled. Besides her nice-ass shape and shoulder-length hair, homegirl was not cute at all, so good for her.

Then Corey, better known as C-God, walked over to the bar. I couldn't believe he was coming over to talk to Tanya. He could have pulled any girl he wanted. C-God was black and ugly, but he had money, confidence, and a cockiness about him that turned me on. He tried to get at me years ago, before the money, but a lot of things have changed since then. He was definitely looking kinda good.

Tanya passed him her number, but judging by the look on his face, I could tell he felt like he had just chosen cake but wanted hot apple pie. I was the pie. It wasn't like he expected me to be here chilling with her. I hadn't seen him in years.

C-God ordered our drinks. He was blinged out, diamonds everywhere—ears, neck, wrist, and pinky finger.

I had my game face on. The eye contact between us was crazy. I wanted him just as bad as he wanted me.

"Damn, somebody must be treating you good, 'cause I remember when you was a toothpick, and you know they say love fattens you up," I said seductively as the alcohol started kicking in.

He flexed his muscles and said, "It ain't fat, baby. It ain't fat at all."

It was getting hot in there, and for every slick little comment I made, he came right back at me with one of his own. I wasn't sure if Tanya caught on or not, but she had to be slow or stupid not to see our chemistry. It was so obvious.

C-God was chilling with his boy Reggie, who must have known what time it was, 'cause he kept Tanya distracted with small talk, while C-God's eyes undressed me, and I loved every bit of it. I wanted his ass right then and there. It wasn't like he was a stranger or anything, I knew him for years in passing. Who cared if Tanya gave him her number? He could do better. He knew it, and so did I. All type of shit was going through my head, and the more I drank, the better he looked.

"Yo, y'all ladies wanna go grab a bite to eat with me and my man?" C-God said, looking in my direction. I smiled and said I was with it.

Since Tanya drove her car, they followed us to her house to park, so we could all ride together. I was hoping the bitch had to work early in the morning so I could roll solo, but Tanya walked right up to C-God's truck and sat up front with him.

Once we got to the diner, she still played him close. I knew what time it was, so I let her have her fifteen minutes of fame. We all laughed, cracked "yo' momma" jokes, and drank some more until the sun was starting to rise.

On the way out, I saw Smitty's punk-ass sitting at a table with some Spanish-looking chick, and there went my high. I hated that muthafucka.

This time Tanya and C-God sat in the back seats on the way home. I rode in the front with Reg. She was all over C-God, and I knew it was only because she felt our vibe. But after seeing Smitty's pussy-stealing-ass, I wasn't in the mood to play any more games. Tanya could have him for now.

Later that morning, I woke up on the wrong side of the bed with a banging-ass headache. I got up to get some Advil when the phone rang. It was Malikai, questioning me with the who, what, why, and where I was all night. He picked the wrong time of day to call and play daddy. I let his ass have it, and before I hung up the phone, I told him not to call me anymore because I was already fucking someone else. I lied, but that was all I could think of to get him mad enough to not want me anymore. Besides, I no longer wanted what was behind door number two. I had my eye on the grand prize.

C-God and I had some unfinished business to tend to. I didn't know how I was gon' make it happen since I didn't have his number, but where there's a will, there is a way.

A week had passed since we all hung out together, and Tanya couldn't wait to let it be known that she was fucking C-God. I was pissed about that whole situation. How the hell did he choose her over me? And I know she enjoyed rubbing that shit in my face. The bitch had the nerve to ask me to hang out with them that night because Reggie had been asking about me. Bullshit! I barely said two words to that nigga. Why would he ask about me?

"Cool, pick me up at ten. I'll roll, 'cause I ain't doing shit else," I said.

Tanya agreed and said she'd see me then. I had something for her ass though. The fat lady ain't sang yet! I pulled out a pair of jeans that hugged my beautiful, round-shaped ass so well that they looked like they was painted on, a black halter top that exposed just the right amount of cleavage, my stiletto boots . . . oh, and let's not forget my brand new Vicki's Secret thong (just in case).

The three of them rolled up to my crib about 10:15, which was cool, because I had just finished touching up my hair and makeup, which was always an earth tone eye shadow and some lip gloss. My father always said real beauty needs no makeup. A man hates to go to bed with a beauty queen and wake up to a monster. Even though I couldn't look like a monster if I tried, I got what he was saying. If it ain't broke, why fix it? Anyway, I hopped in the back of C-God's Escalade and gave Reg a phony, "don't even think about it" smile.

"Hey, girl," I said to Tanya. "What's up, C-God? How you been?"

"Chillin', ma," he responded.

And looking even better than you did the last time, I thought to myself as he constantly watched me from the rearview mirror. C-God knew what was really good, so tonight, I was gonna play the game just to see how it all panned out.

He took us to Night of the Cookers in Brooklyn, which surprised me, because it was a nice, cozy, laid back spot. They had a live band, candlelight, and good food. Money wasn't an issue with C-God. He told us to order what we wanted. Even paid for his broke-ass friend—or should I say broke-ass boy? That's exactly what Reggie was.

Tanya was doing a lot of drinking, as if she was trying to be down or prove something. More power to her, because I wasn't about to get drunk, lose focus, and make a fool of myself.

C-God was so funny, and ain't nothing like a man with money that can make me laugh. Damn, I had to have him. The thought stayed in my head all night. When Tanya got up to go to the ladies room, I couldn't hold it in anymore.

"What's up?" I leaned in closer to C-God. "I know you want me, just 'cause of the way you keep looking at me. So let's stop the game playing and make it happen."

"Aggressive, ain't we? I like that," he said with a smile.

That was it! That was all he had to say, even if he was feeling Tanya. The way he looked at me, it was impossible. I ain't never had to work this hard for no nigga, and I wasn't 'bout to start.

Just then, Tanya came back to the table smelling like she'd been hanging with hurl (throwing up), so we decided to call it a night.

The seating arrangement was different on the way home. Instead of Tanya sitting in the front, C-God told her to take the back seat and Reg was going to sit in the front with him. I was curious to know why, but she didn't question it, and neither did I. Besides, Tanya was wasted and out cold within a matter of seconds.

When we reached my apartment, C-God told Reggie to take the car and make sure Tanya got home safe. I smiled, because I knew it was only a matter of time before he'd come to his senses.

"So, you coming with me?" I asked.

"No doubt." He followed me to my door.

Inside, I decided to set the mood by lighting some aromatherapy candles and turning the radio on to

Vaughn Harper's "The Quiet Storm" on WBLS. I swear the sound of that man's voice could get my panties moist any night of the week.

Before I could say a word, C-God was already undressing me. His body was so hard and muscular, and so was his dick. He worked his tongue from my breasts down to my wet and pulsating pussy and didn't stop working until I reached my climax. I returned the favor, because I had the dick-sucking skills to get a nigga hooked—and of course that was the plan. It wasn't because I was worried about him and Tanya, but because I wanted him all to myself. Besides, he couldn't be stupid enough to go back to burgers after havin' steak.

I gave him the pussy in every position possible: standing up, doggy style, legs up in the air, and even rodeo style. We went at it for hours, until we finally fell asleep. In the morning, I gave him some more.

He had it going on. I swear I had never been with a man that could make my coochie cream the way he did. The only thing that kept interrupting the flow was his cell phone and two-way. They were seriously competing with one another. I wondered if any of those calls were from Tanya, but I didn't ask.

After working up an appetite, we showered off the sex, got dressed, hopped in my car, and went to grab a bite to eat.

I asked him, "What's the status with you and Tanya?" His answer was that she was cool and he fucked her a couple of times, but outside of having a fat ass and nice set of tits, he really wasn't all that attracted to her. He felt I, on the other hand, was the real deal, someone he wouldn't mind kickin' it with, spending a little dough on, or maybe even wifin' me up in a nice condo outside of the hood.

"As long as you good to me, I'm good to you," were his words.

Now, that's what I'm talkin' 'bout! I smiled and asked, "Wasn't I good to you last night?" Joking around with each other was something we both enjoyed doing. Then, he got a call that he couldn't put off and our brunch was cut short.

KEISHA

"Oh, shit!" I screamed as the water started to run down my legs. "Tucker, get up. It's time!" I shouted, waking him out of his sleep with my bag packed and ready to go. I had felt light pains all night the night before, so I packed what I thought I might need to take with me to the hospital early that morning. The real pain hadn't kicked in yet, but all I knew was I was ready to get this little boy out of me and into my arms.

Tucker got up and started to panic more than I was.

"I'm fine. Calm down," I screamed. "Just take me to the hospital."

When we got to the hospital, I was only four centimeters, but they admitted me anyway because my water had already broken. I called up E and Shana because I wanted them to be there. I ended up having to leave messages for both of them.

My sweetie was by my side the whole time, anticipating the arrival of his son. I couldn't ask for a better man. As soon as I had this baby, I was gonna start putting the pressure on him about our wedding plans, before he even thought about taking his ass back out of town. My girls thought I had the perfect situation, but it's always nicer on the outside when you're looking in.

The pains were starting to hit me hard, real hard. I knew it would hurt, but I never imagined like this. Tears fell down the sides of my face, and the love of my life was now my enemy. I didn't want him to touch me;

I didn't want him near me. His voice of support saying, "Push. It's okay," pissed me off even more. He couldn't begin to know what I was feeling.

Ten hours of excruciating pain was finally over, and I was holding the most beautiful baby I had ever seen. Now, all I needed was some sleep.

When I woke up, my room was filled with flowers, teddy bears, and balloons that said "It's a Boy" and "Congratulations." To my surprise, Epiphany and Shana were sitting there watching TV, waiting for me to wake up.

"Hey," I said, still feeling a little tired but excited to see my friends at the same time.

Epiphany smiled and bragged about how cute my baby was. She had jokes, talking about, "I wonder who he got his looks from. He is too cute." I was so glad that she came to see me. She looked so happy. It had to be a new man that had her smiling so much. Tucker told me that she wasn't fucking with Mali anymore.

Shana just stopped by to see me and the baby. She said she couldn't stay because she was working nights now.

"Shana, not *you* with a job. Doing what? It must be illegal," Epiphany said, laughing.

"Well, not everyone needs a man to take care of them," Shana said, not finding Epiphany's comment amusing at all. "I'll come check you when you get home, Keisha."

"What's wrong with her?" E said.

"I don't know, but she looks tired," I said, trying to make an excuse for her attitude.

"I ain't been feeling her," E said. "You know I paged that bitch nine-one-one a couple of times and she never called me back." I just shook my head because I knew how it felt to have a friend not return your calls. "I wonder what kinda job she got anyway. She's probably on the corner selling drugs or something," Epiphany said, being real snobbish.

"That's not nice. Maybe she has a real job, Epiphany. Besides, you guys are friends, so y'all need to stop trippin'," I said.

"I don't know, Keish. You see that little comment she made about me getting money from men? Sounds like jealousy to me. Anyway, speaking of men, girl, remember C-God?" she asked.

"From where?" I asked, not sure whether or not I knew who she was talking about.

"Corey, that used to hang with Walter and Stevie that lived around the corner from us," she said.

"Black-ass Corey Hinderson that used to try and talk to everybody back in the day? Where you see his ugly ass at? I thought he was locked up," I said, disgusted, making her not even want to tell me the rest of her story.

"Well, he's not ugly anymore, and he got money," she said, rolling her eyes at me. Just then, Tucker walked in—perfect timing. Epiphany congratulated him, said good-bye and was out the door.

"What's up, Mommy? Thanks for my little man. He looks just like me," Tucker said.

"You're welcome. You know that was some painful shit, and I just wanted to apologize for being so mean to you."

"It's cool. I know you didn't mean it," Tucker said, accepting my apology.

I kissed his lips. "I love you, and I hope to spend the rest of my life with you, until death do us part." Hint, hint.

SHANA

I swear sometimes Epiphany could just irk the shit out of me, always thinking she was hot shit. Like she was really concerned about where I worked. Shit, now that I thought about it, she was the last person I wanted to know that I danced. I was glad I hadn't tried to plug her ass in, because if she wasn't with it, she was the kind of person that was gonna hate on me for doing it, with her trifling-ass. If I hadn't left when I did, it would've been a girl fight up in there. I was tired of her with that "I'm better then you attitude" and her slick "You from PJs," remarks. That shit was kinda played. On top of all that, I had a helluva hangover, too, so, oh hell yeah, it would've been on in that hospital.

I had gotten my head right at Scar's ladies only party the night before. She had a li'l of this, a li'l of that: cocaine, weed, and e-pills. We called them the "freak-off drugs," 'cause they made you wanna get freaky and downright nasty. Shit, the theme was sex and a good time, and I'd had too much of both that night. I was supposed to be dancing at Honey's tonight, but I was not even in the mood. I called Chasity to see if she wanted to stay home and just chill with me, but she gave me the bullshit about how we needed to go make that money.

She was right, as a matter of fact. I could use the money since I had just spent $200 on a week's worth of Ecstasy. I couldn't dance without them, but I also started taking them just 'cause they made me feel good. Shit, I guess that was their purpose—to make you feel good.

Honey's was packed, but that didn't always mean you were gonna make a lot of money, 'cause fifty percent of the niggas wanted to see the pussy spit fire for a fucking dollar. About twenty percent would come up out their pockets, and the rest of the niggas was straight up trying to get some ass.

A couple of weekends before, this nigga threw beer in my face and demanded his money back. I told him just because he paid me ten dollars for a lap dance didn't mean he could bust off on my ass. I reached for my razor when, lucky for his ass, security came and tossed him out for making a scene. I was 'bout to give his ass a buck fifty slice, to cut him deep until the pink meat was exposed, right across his face.

Nasty bitches like Peaches were having these dudes getting shit twisted, thinking anything went for ten or fifteen dollars. Her anorexic-ass was over in the corner, up against the wall, pretending she was dancing when she was really selling pussy for twenty bucks. The ho knew that shit was against floor rules. That was why we had the champagne room. But niggas didn't be wanting to pay that hundred dollars for those kind of privileges, and the tricks didn't be wanting to give up that twenty percent to the club owner. Shit, I wasn't trying to knock nobody's hustle—and I ain't gon' front, I done sold pussy many a night to get by—but it wasn't what you did, it was how you did it, and these hoes was fucking up the game.

As I squeezed my way through the funky little changing room/bathroom to get dressed, or should I say undressed, I overheard two strippers named Mahogany and Diamond whispering that some baller was out there tricking off a knot of cash and buying out the bar. That shit was music to my ears. I was scheduled to dance some stage sets tonight, so I wouldn't have to give Billy twenty dollars. He was the owner, and he charged twenty dollars to all the dancers that just came to lap dance, and paid seventy dollars to the dancers that got on stage and danced for three sets. Fuck that. I made arrangements to trade places with this girl Silk so I could try to milk this nigga they was talking about before my stage performance.

"Chasity, hurry up. There's money out there, girl," I said.

"You ain't said nothin' but a word. Let's go." She smiled.

The deejay was playing my song, "There's Some Hoes in This House." It wasn't hard to figure out where the real money was, because the hoes flocked to him like he was Jay-Z shooting a video for "Girls, Girls, Girls." Only thing wrong with this video was that most of the bitches in here looked like "who done it and why." I mean, they were tore up from the floor up, so it wouldn't be hard to steal the nigga's attention.

Chasity's pretty-ass was a big flirt anyway, and a hustler, like me. Automatically, a scheme came into play, 'cause great minds do think alike. The plan was to get him to spend some money here, then hit a telli (motel) on some two-for-the-price-of-one type shit, fuck him to sleep, and rob his ass.

"Would you like a dance?" Chasity asked him.

"Nah, I'm good, but what up with you and your girl giving my man here a dance? It's his birthday."

After like five drinks, I lost count as far as how many dances we gave his boy. I also changed the plan about trying to rob dude. I was feeling him a li'l something. I was feeling him even more when he peeled off four hundred-dollar bills from the money stashed in his right pocket and gave me and Chass two hundred a piece.

"I didn't get your name," I said with a smile.

"That's because I didn't give it. What's yours?" he said, showing his pearly whites. "Sha—I mean, Cream," I said, almost giving up my government.

Chocolate boy wonder wasn't giving up nothing else but a smile. "I'll be back to check you, shorty," he said as he got up from the bar to leave.

I hit him back with a quick response. "I'll be waiting." It was only 1:00 a.m. I had a couple of hundreds in my pocket and still three hours left to dance my sets and make some more. Shit, I wasn't mad at all.

"Chasity, did you get dude's name?" I asked.

"Nah, but his boy's name is Mike. He gave me his number."

"Oh, really," I said with a li'l hate in my tone.

EPIPHANY

I dozed off watching the amateur night part of the Apollo when the phone rang and woke me. I debated on whether or not I should answer or let my machine pick it up. I looked at the caller ID and decided to answer.

"Yo, what up, ma? What you doing?"

"Who's this?" I said, knowing exactly who it was.

"Damn, after all the good-ass pussy you been giving me, you still don't know who dis is?" he said.

"Oh, hey, C-God. What's up, baby?"

"I hope you and me, 'cause I'm in front of your crib."

"So what, you tryin' to come in?"

"Oh, no doubt, but for now why don't you throw on something and come take a ride with me?"

"All right. I'll be out in five minutes," I said. I jumped up and threw on a pair of Gap jeans, a baby tee, and a pair of Chanel shoes, then ran to the bathroom, took off my head scarf, and combed down my wrap. I brushed my teeth and put a little Oh Baby M·A·C gloss on my lips, with liner, of course.

When I got out to his truck, he was in the passenger's seat. I assumed he wanted me to drive.

"So, where we going?" I asked.

"Let's go get something to eat, 'cause a nigga starvin'."

I wasn't really hungry, but I could tell C had been drinking, so maybe a little food would sober him up. I suggested Georgia Peach, this diner on Queens Boulevard. He already had his eyes closed and seat leaning all the way back. I guess it was left up to me.

"Hey, wake up. I'm gonna just go place your order to go. What do you want?" I said.

"Order me some chicken fingers and fries."

After getting his food, I drove back to my place. He came in and fell out on my bed.

Two months had passed since I started fucking around exclusively with C, and to my surprise, I wasn't even tired of him yet. We had lots of fun together. He seemed to be doing all the right things. Not only did he give up that paper willingly, but he made me feel like I was the sexiest bitch to ever walk the planet. Sometimes, we would just take a late night ride, smoke some trees, and listen to slow jams. I felt safe with him.

Niggas knew not to fuck with him. He had a reputation for murdering niggas in a heartbeat, friend or foe. That was hard for me to believe because I hadn't seen that side of him yet, although I did hear him talking on his cell to his boy Mike about some cat that had the Carolinas and Virginia on lock and was selling his weight for cheap prices, so his clientele was large.

"Yo, I want you and Ness to keep an eye on that nigga. Find out who else he down with, 'cause that nigga trying to stop me from eating, yo, and it ain't gon' happen, son. What, yo! Just do what the fuck I said and holla back from a pay phone. A'ight, out!"

I walked in the room right as he slammed the hood down on his Nextel, feeling kind of turned on by his authority.

"What up, ma?" he asked.

"I'm about to show you," I said as I kneeled down on my knees and unzipped his pants. I began to deep throat his thick ten and a half inches of hardness.

"Um, damn, that's what's up. You tryin' to turn a nigga out or something? Don't stop," he moaned and moaned some more.

I knew I had him right where I wanted him. His body started to jerk as he clutched on to the edge of the bed and began to breathe heavy. "Oh, shit. I'm about to cum," he said. Normally at that point I would have stopped, but his excitement made my pussy start to cum as well, so instead of stopping, I drank them babies.

"C, next weekend my girl Keisha—you remember Keisha, right?"

"Yeah, she kinda short, brown skin, right?"

"Uh-huh, that's her."

"Who she fuck with?" he inquired.

"This guy named Tucker."

"From where?" he continued.

"He's from Brooklyn, but they live together out here in Jamaica. Anyway, listen. She's baptizing their son, and I'm gonna to be the godmother. You wanna come with me?"

"Nah, that ain't my type of party," he said.

I got a little attitude. Shit, after one of my best head jobs, "No" was not what I wanted to hear. As those thoughts ran through my mind, he must've noticed the disappointment on my face, because he started explaining his reason.

"Churches just make me feel uncomfortable, so don't be mad, a'ight." Then he said those magic words: "You need some money?"

"Yeah," I said with a smile.

"How much you need?" he asked.

"About five hundred."

"A'ight, I got you," he said, holding me tight. "So, what's good for the night? You wanna go out for a drink?"

This boy knew he could drink. Since I'd been fuckin' with him, I'd become a bit of a lush my damn self. I thought before I said, "Sounds like a plan to me."

Later that night we hit this spot on Merrick called Quiet Storm. I'd lived in south side Jamaica all my life, and I never knew Queens had so many local hangout spots.

C-God sat at the bar, and I went to the bathroom. The place was small but packed. As I walked to the back to look for the bathroom, I noticed there were more women then men. I mean, it had to be like five women to one man: a perfect example of how there's a shortage of men in the world. On my way back to the bar, I heard the deejay say, "Free drinks for the first twenty-five ladies. Oh yeah, ladies, you got ten minutes to place your drink order."

You should've seen those thirsty bitches pushing each other as they ran over and bum-rushed the bar. The shit was crazy. It reminded me of the way them old ladies in my neighborhood be rushing to the church every Wednesday morning to get that free bag of food before it ran out. I wasn't even tryin' to take a chance getting back to the bar, 'cause if one of those thirsty hoes stepped on my $300 boots from Sacco's, it was gonna be on up in there. So I waited out the ten minutes.

Then the deejay stopped the music again and said, "Oh yeah, ladies, those drinks . . . compliments from my man C-God over there at the bar. Ha ha! I see ya, big baller. Y'all ladies thank him for quenching that thirst, a'ight. My man, this song's for you, player."

The deejay was giving C props. He threw on Jay-Z's "Big Pimpin'."

I was pissed. I couldn't believe this nigga was up in there spending money on those bitches, money that could've been spent on me. I squeezed my ass right through the crowd that had now loosened up a little. All I seen was girls up in his face smiling, and his ass enjoying every moment of it. Oh, he was really tryin'a play me.

"Excuse me," I said in a nasty tone.

"Oh, this my baby right here, ladies. Say hello," he said to the birds standing around him then turned to me. "You a'ight, ma? I got us a bottle of Mo. They ain't got the good stuff." I couldn't believe this nigga was on some real pimp shit, talking 'bout "This my baby, ladies. Say hello," like these skank-ass bitches really cared.

"To answer your question, no, I'm not a'ight. I'm ready to go."

"Come on, ma. I'm just having a little fun. Besides, ain't none of these hoes drinking what you drinking."

"Oh, so that makes it a'ight?"

"Yeah, it do. We came together, and we leaving together, so drink the champagne and stop trippin'."

I did what he said, while he continued to flirt and acknowledge my presence at the same time. I was so pissed off. Besides his money, I made him look good, so for him to sit there and play me was fucked up. I could have had any nigga I wanted, and I chose him. None of those hoes looked better than me. I repeated this in my head over and over again to build my shattered confidence back up. Then I spotted Shana and some girl on the dance floor. That was my cue to break away for a minute.

"C-God, I'll be back." I got up and walked over to say what's up. Shana was high as hell. She introduced me to her friend Chasity, who from the looks of it seemed to have straight attitude toward me, which I ignored. I didn't have much to say to Shana, and neither did she. You would have never guessed that we were—or should

I say *used to be* best friends. I asked if she was going to Keisha's son's christening, and if so, I'd see her there. I felt kinda awkward, so I used that as my cue to move along.

Just as I was about to go look for Mr. Don Fuckin' Juan, he found me.

I noticed Shana's eyes light up from the sight of C-God, so I didn't even bother to introduce them to each other. I grabbed his hand and just walked off.

On the way back to my house, I let C-God have it. I told him he better not ever try to fuckin' play me like that again. He apologized too easily and promised to make it up to me.

When we pulled up in front of my place, he told me he couldn't stay because he had some business to take care of. He said he'd see me the next day. I planted a wet one on those thick lips of his, said good night, and went inside my house.

Maybe I was tripping just a little. Shit, what the fuck was a few six-dollar drinks compared to my rent, my car note, and the five or six hundred he kept in my pocket for me to spend? I thought as I lay in the bed and drifted off into a sound sleep.

EPIPHANY

"Epiphany, pick up the phone. Hello? Hello." My mother's voice coming from the answering machine woke me up out of my sleep.

"Yeah, Ma!" I said as I picked up and glanced at the clock that read 12:00 p.m.

"Why are you still sleeping? Still hanging out until late night, huh?"

"Mommy, come on. Is that what you called me for?" I asked.

"No, I called because you're my only child and I don't think I need a reason to call you. Even though you're grown, I still worry about you, you know. I also worry about your choice of men."

"Huh." I let out a deep sigh, hoping she wasn't gon' take it there, but she did.

"Listen, Epee, your father and I worry about you, whether you like it or not. When we heard that you were running around with that loser, I couldn't believe that my daughter would settle for such trash. He ain't no good, and I got a bad feeling about you being with him.

"Now, listen, Epee, you know that I love me a thug too, but it will catch up to you. I've been through so much as a young girl dealing with your father, but he always put family first, and he kept us out of harm's way at all times. That's why I stayed with him. These li'l niggas out here nowadays ain't got that sense of family. All they know is shooting up shit and going back and forth to jail. Your father had a plan. He used the negative and turned it to a positive by taking his money, making investments, and turning his shit legit. He didn't run around killing and making babies all over the place. He took care of home."

"Mommy, I don't wanna hear it. Daddy hustled in the streets for years. I remember. So what, you tryin'a tell me he ain't never came across a life or death situation where it was either him or his enemy's life in jeopardy? If so, I don't believe it. Killing comes with the territory."

"Your father ain't no killer. Don't you ever come out your face to me about him like that. He's always been there for you and me both. He's still paying for your shit every month, young lady. You need to recognize when shit is too good. You're an adult now. He doesn't have to take care of you the way he does, Miss Thang, so think about that, okay?" she said in a nasty, like-she-just-let-me-have-it tone.

After that I lost it 'cause I felt like whatever they did for me, they owed me. No matter what they ever gave me, they couldn't give me back my virginity. I started to scream at her.

"Look, Daddy's there for you, Mommy. Yeah, he might put a check in the mail every month for me, but where was he when I really needed him? He was too busy wining and dining and taking you on trips, while Uncle Ramel was fuc—just forget it. I gotta go!" Almost in tears and ready to let the cat out the bag, I slammed the phone down.

KEISHA

Tucker wasn't happy about me wanting Epiphany to be our son's godmother. For the past three months, all he had kept saying was, "You sure about that? 'Cause that trick ain't cut out for the job. The only person Epiphany thinks about is herself. Look how she played my man out. Matter of fact, look how she played you when you was pregnant."

"I know Epiphany ain't big on kids, but she's my best friend, and regardless of what you think, that girl was there for me when I didn't have you. What about Malikai's ass? He ain't no fucking angel, but you don't hear me tripping out. So what is this really about? What got you so salty toward my friend? Is it because she dropped your boy?" I said, defending my friend. Tucker just looked at me and didn't say a word.

The ceremony was beautiful, despite how Tucker or Mali might have felt about Epiphany. Everyone handled themselves like adults. Thank God!

Malikai had brought his new girl, or should I say one of them. Shana didn't even show up, and I didn't bother to ask Epiphany about Corey. I was sure she had her reasons for not bringing him.

After the baptism, we all decided to head out to Manhattan to celebrate over an early dinner. I was surprised but happy when E agreed to come along. I thought being around Malikai and his friend would've made her uncomfortable, but that wasn't the case. Actually, the way Mali kept watching Epiphany might have made his date feel a little out of place.

We reached home around eight o'clock. After bathing my li'l man, giving him a warm bottle, and finally getting him to sleep, the next thing I did was call Shana to make sure she was okay. I paged her three times before calling her house.

"Hi, Ms. Pat. Is Shana there?"

"No. Who's calling?"

"I'm sorry, Ms. Pat. This is Keisha."

"Oh, hi, sweetie. How's your little bundle of joy doing?"

"He's doing good. I just put him to bed."

"That's good. When you gon' bring him by to see me?" Ms. Pat asked.

"Soon, real soon. Can you please tell that girl to call me?"

"I will when I see her."

"What, she don't live there no more?" I asked.

"Barely. That child stay in them damn streets, and when she here, she got some nigga ringing my telephone all times of the night. I guest he her man or something. I don't know, 'cause I ain't never seen him. All I do know is when he call, she's out the door like a bat out of hell."

"Well, what about her night job?" I asked, 'cause Ms. Pat will tell it all.

"What job? Shaking her naked tail for them perverts. Shit, that ain't no job."

"Ms. Pat, she's dancing now?"

"Now? She's been doing that for a while. She didn't tell you?"

"No!" I said, surprised.

"Yeah, she's been dancing with some new girlfriend of hers."

"What girl?"

"I don't know, but she ain't from around here. I think her name is Cassidy," Ms. Pat answered. "What, y'all ain't friends no more?"

"Of course we're friends. I've just been tied up with the baby, that's all."

"Well, that's good you ain't out in them streets, 'cause ain't nothing out there but trouble. I'm through talking. I done washed my hands with Shana. She just gon' have to find out what's out there the hard way."

"Okay, Ms. Pat, just tell her I called, please."

"Like I said, when I see her, I'll tell her. You take care now. Bye."

Whew, that lady knew she could do some talking! Damn, talking to Shana's mother made me really start to worry about her. I just prayed my friend was okay.

Tucker came out of the bathroom smelling so fresh and so clean. He must have been feeling the family thing, 'cause he laid his head on my lap and said, "Keish, you know I love you, right, baby?" I nodded. "We got us a fly li'l man. He looks just like his pops. So, let's just do the damn thing. Be my wife. That's all I want from you. We gon' do it up big, too," he said proudly. I was speechless and at the same time trying to hold back my tears.

"Keish, I'm getting tired of this lifestyle I'm living. I got enough money stashed to take us up outta here, anywhere you want to go, and to hold us over for a while. So, think about it, Keish. I'm serious. I promise you after I make these last couple of moves this hustling shit is a wrap."

I couldn't hold back my tears of joy any longer. I'd been praying for that moment. I kissed his lips and made love to him like never before. Everything was falling right into place, I thought in silence, and before I closed my eyes, I thanked God for answering my prayers. I asked Him to look after my two best friends.

EPIPHANY

On the bright side of things, I thought I might be in love with C-God. That shit was crazy. When we were together, I swear the nigga gave me butterflies. He was definitely the first out of many. I'd never had a man that took pleasure in stimulating my body the way he did. I mean, I never had a nigga that just concentrated on satisfying the pussy without just trying to get a nut. You feel me?

One night, I had a dream that I was having his seed, and I woke up happy thinking about the possibilities. Now, you know his shit was good if I woke up hoping to become baby momma number six. Yep, six babies and five mommas. Now, that's five times the drama for your ass. That was part of the not-so-bright side of what I'm talking 'bout, 'cause when there is a bright side of any relationship, there is a dark side that follows, and everybody has one.

Lately, everything had been, "Yo, I gotta go take care of some business, so I can't stay long," or "I might be back, I might not." What type of shit was that? I'll tell you exactly what it was: it was some man-shit for your ass. You see, before they get you, they gotta have you no matter what it takes. But once they get you, the thrill is gone and you become just another piece of pussy.

One night, I got a call from Bay, this older Jamaican cat who was still in the game. He hustled weed. We got up every now and then on the low . . . no public appearances, because he looks like a monster—a monster with money coming out his ass. Bay would trick off hundreds just to eat my pussy and that's all. I would let him, but it didn't turn me on at all. I mean literally, he really did look scary, and on top of that, his uncircumcised dick looked like a fucking oversized anteater.

On the real, though, Bay was the kind of trick that you'd want to keep around, because there were times when all I had to do was call him up, kick some "I miss you" bullshit for some cash, and he'd give it up.

In his strong Jamaican accent, he ran his game. "Baby girl, where ya been? I miss yer sweet stuff. Come, let me see you and take you shopping."

"Oh, yeah. When would you like to do all of that?" I asked.

"Tomorrow, baby," he responded.

Of course my answer was yes, 'cause I didn't turn down money or shopping. We set up a date to meet around 1:00 p.m. at the Cheesecake Factory in Long Island. Yeah, yeah, yeah, I know I said I didn't like being seen with him, but it was either that or meeting up at his house. Besides, I already had it planned out: after we grabbed a bite, he'd give me some cash, and I'd tell the nigga that I was on my period or something, 'cause Jamaicans don't run those kind of red lights.

I woke up that morning, checking my caller ID. I fell asleep the night before waiting on C to call me back after paging and calling his ass around three or four times. There were no calls from him, so I paged him again. That was the bullshit I hated: that inconsiderate shit that came with fucking with a drug dealer. You never knew what was going on in the streets when a nigga didn't call you back. Three things came to mind: *I hope he ain't somewhere shot the fuck up, locked up, or out fucking some other bitch.* Shit, I know it sounds fucked up, but I'd rather his ass be dead or locked up than for him to be out somewhere screwing some other ho.

I called Keisha to push back the time that I was coming to scoop my godson for a couple of hours, while she went to enroll in school. Things had been so cool between us, and I was surprisingly loving the godmommy thing more and more.

"Hold on, Keisha. Somebody's on my other line," I told her. It was C calling with some bullshit excuse about how he was so busy last night that he forgot to call, and his battery was dead on his cell phone. Yeah, whatever. I'd heard it all before, I said to myself, while he kept going on and on with excuses.

"Okay, C, let me go, 'cause I'm on my way to Keisha's," I said with an attitude. He didn't know he just gave me a reason to go see Bay and not feel guilty about it.

"Yo, where she live at again?" C-God inquired.

"What you mean, where she live at again? I never told you before where she lived at in the first place, and what's with all the questions lately about my girl and her man? You checking for her or something?" I asked heatedly.

"Nah, boo, I was just gonna stop by her crib and hit you with some of this dough I was busy getting last night, that's all."

"Well, when I get home, I'll call you, then you can come over and we can both hit each other off. Okay, daddy?" He liked when I called him daddy.

"Yeah, a'ight then. See you later. Be good. One."

I wasn't trying to be on no jealous shit, but C had been asking me a lot of fucking questions about Keisha and Tucker. If it wasn't Keisha he was interested in, then it must have had something to do with her man. Whatever it was, I didn't want no parts of it.

Speaking of Keisha, I clicked back over to her holding on my other line and made sure she was cool with the time change. "Girl, don't be late," she yelled as we were hanging up.

I took a quick shower, threw on my Juicy jeans and matching jacket and some Timbs, and put my hair in a ponytail. I didn't want to look too good for Bay's ass, which was hard to do even when I dressed down, but who's complaining?

I arrived at the restaurant around 1:15, which was cool since I didn't want to seem anxious anyway. The wait was always long at this restaurant, but the food was good.

There was no sign of Bay, so I decided to give my name to the hostess. She said there was a twenty minute wait.

At 1:30, I called Bay's cell phone but got no answer. I kept calling until some Jamaican woman, who sounded like she was crying, answered his cell. She gave me the third degree before she told me he was dead. She said she found her brother this morning. He was shot in the head, and whoever did this didn't know who they was messing with. Her other brothers were on their way from Kingston, Jamaica, and they were gonna "lick up every bomboclot until they find the one who did this."

"Epiphany, table for two, your table is ready," the hostess announced over the loudspeaker. I told Bay's sister I was sorry for her loss and that he was a good friend to me and I hoped they found the bastards that did it.

"Last call for Epiphany, table for two," was all I heard as I walked out of the restaurant.

Damn, I couldn't believe Bay was dead. I really wanted those Prada shoes and matching bag. I guess C was gonna have to buy them for me now.

I felt bad, so I went and bought myself a Louis Vuitton bag and a bottle of Donna Karen's Cashmere Mist perfume to make myself feel better. I hope I don't sound too shallow. I just do what works for me.

KEISHA

Epiphany had been such a big help to me with my son. She was my sista for life. Now, as far as Shana went, I didn't know what was up with that girl. After leaving several messages with her mom, I still hadn't heard from her. All I knew was that she was still alive, and Ms. Pat said if that should change, she'd let me know. In other words, I guess that meant stop calling so much.

I finally got around to enrolling back in school for my master's. Tucker thought I should wait until we moved, but why put off for later what could be done now? Besides, I was hoping maybe he'd hold off on moving until I finished. I honestly didn't know why we had to move anyway.

Tucker had been in and out of town like a madman. I knew these were the final moves before his retirement, so as long as he kept the lines of communication open, I tried not to complain. Now that I was back in school, I'd have more to do with my time. I was still planning my wedding.

Even though Shana had been M.I.A. I still had faith in her and our friendship; however, I had already asked Lea, a good friend of mines that I met in college, to take her place if I should need a Plan B. I had no choice; the bridal shop needed everyone's measurements as soon as possible. I also made arrangements for my younger sisters to be in my wedding.

This was going to be a very special day, because not only was I marrying my man, but I hadn't seen my sisters in about six years. They were nine and eleven the last time I saw them. I had to bribe my Nana with a couple of dollars for her to agree to it, but what the hell . . .? Money makes the world go 'round.

I was so excited. Tucker and I had already come up with 150 people on our guest list and counting. Once again, Epiphany and Malikai had to put up with each other, because he was the best man and she was my maid of honor. I told her jokingly that she should have stayed with him, because she saw him more now than when they were together!

The catering hall that I chose was so beautiful, and once we filled it with white roses, an ice sculpture of kissing doves, a seafood salad bar, top shelf open bar stocked with Cristal, a popular deejay spinning the records, and all our family and close friends, it was gonna be a day to remember. Oh, and I forgot to mention Tucker was planning to have me serenaded by one of my favorite singers. I had so many, but I was hoping it was Gerald Levert. He wouldn't tell me who, so I guess we'd just have to wait and see.

Ring, ring.

My cell phone snapped me right out of my wedding plans. It was Tucker calling. There had to be some drama, 'cause that was the only time he called my cell. Tucker never discussed the game on the home phone.

"Hello," I answered, hoping everything was okay.

"Hey, Keish," he said on the other end, sounding a little stressed out.

"What's wrong? And when are you coming home? We miss you."

"Keish, I miss you guys too. I can't wait to hold you in my arms. I wanted to send for you and little man, but some kids that I fuck with down here just got knocked, so shit is a little crazy right now. I gotta hit his people off with a little bail money, and then I should be back up that way by Saturday night. I love you. Gotta go." He hung up before I could respond.

I swear I couldn't wait until this shit was over so we could live a normal life. I spent so much time worrying and praying to God to keep my man safe that it was starting to drive me nuts. I even started a trust fund for the baby and stashed away over fifty G's in a safety deposit box, and let's not mention the million dollar life insurance policy just in case, God forbid, something happened to Tucker. Lord only knows. I hated to think like that, but this shit scared me.

EPIPHANY

It was the first time I'd seen C-God sniff coke. "Yo, boo, you want some? It'll make the sex a lot better," he said.

"Nah. I don't fuck with that shit."

Then he had the nerve to say I wasn't no fun. Shit, I didn't think my sex needed any improvement. This nigga was trippin'. For one, I barely sas him anymore and then his wife had the nerve to call my house the other night talking 'bout I better leave her man alone. That's right, his so-called wife. I didn't even know he had one of those.

Unfortunately for her, he was eating my pussy when she called; therefore, I even didn't trip. I just passed him the phone. The only reason I was certain that it was over between them was because of what he said and the hateful way he screamed at her when he said, "Yo, ain't nothin' wrong with my seeds, right? Then what the fuck I tell you? If they a'ight, then don't be fuckin' calling me for no bullshit, and don't call my girl's house no fuckin' more either, understand?"

I asked him how she got my number. He didn't know the answer to that question. Then I asked him why he didn't tell me he was married.

"'Cause the bitch is crazy." He explained that she only called herself his wife because she had two kids by him, so the bitch felt special.

I let the shit go, 'cause she couldn't possibly be that stupid to let him talk to her like that and still be fuckin' with him. I gave them both the benefit of the doubt. Plus, I knew he'd been stressed out lately, and I wasn't trying to add on to it.

A lot of C's stress was because the nigga didn't believe in using condoms, and now half his baby's mommas wanted to take him to court for child support. As far as him hustling, his product must not have been moving too well, 'cause lately he hadn't been spending money like he used to. Now he was breaking the number one rule of the drug game: Getting high on his own supply.

"C, what's up? Is everything okay?" I asked.

"I'm good," he said.

"You sure? 'Cause I didn't know you was getting high."

"What the fuck is you talking 'bout, getting high? Shit, every muthafucka out there hustling fuck with li'l girl every now and then. You don't be complaining when you getting this stiff dick up in you, huh, thanks to this shit right here," he said, sounding very irritated.

"Listen, calm down, I just didn't know, C-God. I barely see you anymore," I said, feeling a little intimidated by his tone.

"Well, I can't fuck with you all the time. A nigga gotta make money, especially since you be in my fucking pockets all the time. So don't start beating me in my fuckin' head 'bout what the fuck I do with my time, 'cause I'ma start dismissing bitches and niggas, who-ever trying to stop me from getting that paper. That's my word, niggas don't know. I want it all, and if I gotta start killing muthafuckas for it, then that's what it's gon' be. These niggas is out here pushing fly-ass whips, bouncing in and out of town and shit like they the kings of fucking New York. They 'bout to get it, and they ain't even gonna see it coming. On that note, yo, I'm out. I got moves to make." C-God grabbed his pint of Remy V.S.O.P. and headed out my front door.

I started to assume shit. Could he be talking about Malikai and Tucker? They were out of town a lot, and Tucker did push a 745LI BMW, SL500 Mercedes, and a Range Rover. Mali just had his Navigator truck. With all the questions C was asking me about Keisha, it was possible.

I didn't know what to do. If I told Tucker and Mali to watch their backs, then C might fuck me up, and I wasn't trying to have that happen. Besides, what if I was wrong? I was sure there were other niggas out there getting money in and out of town. I was just gonna mind my business.

It had been two weeks since C-God walked out talking shit that night. He hadn't called me, and I hadn't called him. Part of me missed him and his money. The other part just didn't want to fuck with him anymore because of the way he acted.

I'd been over Keisha's crib a lot lately, helping her get the wedding together, and neither she nor Tucker mentioned any possible beef with C-God. Keisha knew I was fucking with him, so believe me, if there was some drama involving Tucker, she would have said something to me about it by now.

Watching Keisha and Tucker all over each other, kissing and laughing, made me miss C-God more and more. We had good times, too, and maybe I should've been easy, knowing the stress he'd been going through.

When I got in my car to head home, the first thing I did was call him. I didn't want to call the cell, so I just left a message on his two-way, telling him how much I missed him. That way if he felt the same, he'd hit me back.

In less than two minutes after leaving that message, my cell was ringing. It was C calling me back. He apologized for the way he'd acted. He said the only reason he didn't call me was because he felt like maybe he might have turned me off when I seen him sniff coke. He assured me that it wasn't a habit, and if I was uncomfortable with it, he promised to not even fuck around with it.

Then he said, "You know I love you, baby girl."

A big Kool-Aid smile grew across my face as I said, "I love you back. Now, can you meet me at my house and give me some of that stiff dick?"

"I'm on my way," he replied.

SHANA

I knew it had to be Epiphany that called and had him flying outta there. If it was one of his babies' mommas or business, he would've talked in front of me. He told me about their argument, but I guess all that talk about him not fucking with her boring-ass anymore was just a bunch of bullshit. I wasn't stressing it, 'cause I was the one laying up in his crib, making runs with him, counting his money, moving 500 X pills a week at Honey's for his ass, and fucking him any way he wanted it. I was that down-ass bitch that a thug-ass nigga needed by his side.

So, if he wanted to fuck with Epiphany still, I was't gon' sweat it, 'cause he dropped her ass off for a reason and came back to Quiet Storm that night to holla at me. When I seen him with Epiphany, I was just gonna fall back, but her nigga chose me, so like Snoop Dog said, "It ain't no fun if my homie can't have none." Let the games begin; for once the shoe was on the other foot.

The shit I had put up with from Epiphany all these years, she had better be glad all I was doing was fucking her man. I should've beat her ass on several occasions a long time ago. Like that time when we were seventeen and she fucked Curtis Jacobson just to get back at his boy Dre for doing her dirty. She knew I was crazy about Curtis. I used to love the ground that boy walked on, and even though he wasn't feeling me, she still violated our friendship rule. Talk about being hurt; I was crushed, but I let it slide.

Then there were times where she used to try and play me around a bunch of niggas 'cause I ain't have as much as she did, so the bitch would give me clothes—nice shit she didn't want and Keisha couldn't fit. Around guys, Epiphany always got a lot of the attention, but that wasn't enough. She'd say shit like, "Girl, them jeans I gave you fit nice. Did the other things fit good too?" Like the ho ain't seen me all fucking day to ask me that shit in private. I would get so embarrassed, until I got used to it. Keisha would always do what Epiphany told her to do, but I wasn't having that bullshit, and she couldn't stand it.

The girl had something against people who lived in the projects too. She thought she was better, but if her father didn't hustle hard to get that house in a neighborhood that was still the hood, she'd probably be my next-door neighbor.

What it all boiled down to was this: I had enough of her, and even though Keisha never did anything but look out for me, she was Epiphany's friend first. The bitch barely came to see her when she was knocked up, but who did she ask to be the godmother and maid of honor? Not me. It was best that I just kept my distance from both of them bitches for a while.

I picked up the phone to call Chasity. I'd been so caught up with C-God that I hadn't really been fucking with her. I knew she was mad.

"Hello," Chasity answered.

"What's up, Chass? I miss you."

"Oh yeah, you miss me now? So is this how it's gonna be every time you get a little dick in your life? What, you just gon' push me off to the side?" she asked.

"Listen, C-God and my relationship is not just about sex, and you need to stop trippin' 'cause it ain't like I don't put you down. You enjoy getting high for free and his dick too. Me and you is me and you, but I told you from the door, dick and hustling is something I ain't never giving up," I said, setting the record straight.

"So he be paying you?" Chasity asked.

"Hell yeah. That's the only reason why I ain't been coming to Honey's to dance. I be in the bathroom pushing that Dr. Feelgood hard, 'bout three hundred or more Ecstasy pills at thirty dollars a pop in less than a week. That's nine G's, and out of that I get a bullshit li'l fifteen hundred. But I need his ass right now, 'cause I'm trying to get my own hustle going through his connect. I'm stacking my dough, too, so I can get a whip and come pick you up from the club sometimes. But anyway, what's up for tonight? Let's go hang out," I suggested, knowing that would increase the peace between us.

"A'ight, there's this nice all-girl spot on the west side of Manhattan," Chasity said.

"That's what's up. I'll meet you there at eleven."

EPIPHANY

If I had known a couple of weeks apart would have made shit this good between me and C-God, I would have started a fight with him when he first started to fuck up. We were hanging out in the city that night. I was gonna rock my leather jumpsuit because it hugged the hell out of my curves, and with the chinchilla fur jacket that C just bought me, that shit just added more fuel to my fire.

Business must have picked up for him, because he was definitely splurging again. Since we had been back together, he'd been handling a lot of business over the phone and spending every night in my bed. I hadn't picked up my phones or checked my answering machine that read "full" in days. There had been no need to. I had what I wanted right there.

I grabbed the phone and called up Walk That Walk Salon to speak to Ardie (girlfriend knew he could do some hair) to see if he would squeeze me in his morning schedule, which I was sure was already tight. After he cursed me out for missing my last appointment three months ago, he agreed by saying, "You better not be late."

I hated driving all the way to Harlem to get my hair done, but it was worth it. I got up, threw on some clothes, and set off the automatic starter on my car so it could warm up because it was cold outside. I walked into the bedroom and woke up C-God to let him know

I was on my way to my hair appointment. I knew he probably would use that as an opportunity to go take care of some business. I kissed his lips and told him I'd see him later.

When I arrived at the salon, Ardie snatched me up as soon as I signed in, and started my wash. I told him I wanted something a little different than my usual.

"Miss Thing, I know you ain't trying to cut all this pretty hair."

"No, I don't want to cut it, but maybe add some color."

"Oh, 'cause I was fixin' to say, girl, I'll cut the hell out of it. Humph, you'll still be a diva either way, but don't worry, girl. I got you," he said.

I wasn't worried, because Ardie was the best, and three hours later, a few shades lighter, and a couple of streaks, I was definitely feeling fierce. I even tipped girlfriend fifty dollars, which was a stretch from the usual fifteen. I felt too cute to go home just yet, so I headed to Macy's on Thirty-fourth to do a little shopping.

I reached home a little after six and called C on his cell to let him know that I was home. Then I decided to check the messages on my cell and answering machine. Most of my calls were from Keisha. She was calling to see if I was okay, because she hadn't heard from me. There were also two messages from my dad, calling to tell me and remind me about the big bash he was throwing for my Mom's fortieth birthday, which was the next day.

Oh, shit! I had forgotten all about her birthday. I spoke to her after we had that argument, but that was over a month ago. I quickly dialed my father's cell phone and gave him a song and dance about how I was working as a customer service rep for a cellular phone company and my hours had been hectic. That was why I took so long to get back to him, but I would be there, and if he needed me to bring anything, he should just let me know.

Daddy always seemed to fall for whatever I told him, but not this time. I sensed some real anger in his voice.

"I know you're grown, but your mother and I feel you should come around or call more often than you do. I've been calling you for damn near three weeks and you're just getting back to me. Anything could have been wrong, Epee. This shit has to stop. The only time we hear from you is when you need something, and since that job is keeping you so busy, let him pay your car note and your rent from now on. I'll see you at the party." *Click*. A dial tone was all I heard.

I couldn't believe he'd just said that to me. Shit, I didn't need him or his money, and what he didn't know was any job I was fucking with was paying my bills. Daddy's check went straight to the bank. Shit, that was one thing Mommy did do right. She ain't raise no fool. She always told me to get it while the getting was good, so when it stopped, I'd have. And that's exactly what I did. I deposited the check Daddy gave me every month in the bank. Then, when it cleared, I withdrew it and put it in my safety deposit box. Keisha put me on to the safety deposits, because if you have more than $10,000 in the bank, they will report it to the IRS, and then they'll be all up in your business. So to avoid that, a deposit box was better. I ain't gonna say how much I had saved up, but let's just say if it ever rained or poured, I was good!

C-God rolled up in front of my place just before midnight with his boy Mike, who hated me for whatever reason. From the look on his face, he wasn't too happy about me hanging out with the fellas tonight. I could tell, 'cause the nigga even hesitated like he had some shit to think about before he gave up the front seat.

Let me tell you about this nigga Mike. He was one of them arrogant-ass niggas, mad at the world, but especially at women.

"Man, them chicks is all the same, only good for fucking, or getting fucked up for fucking up. I'll beat a bitch ass in a minute. I don't give a fuck. Them ho-bitches know not to fuck with me." That's the type of shit that came out of Mike's mouth.

Unfortunately, he was C-God's right-hand man, basically just another "do boy." He was a hot-headed li'l twenty-year-old with a happy trigger finger. He would go all out for C, 'cause C-God had been looking out for Mike since he was a li'l nigga. Nevertheless, the feelings were mutual, because I couldn't stand his ass either.

When we got to the club, the place was pretty small. It must have been an exclusive spot, because from the outside it didn't even look like a club. The music was hot to death, and you had to be on balla status just to get in the spot. I mean, you could only sit at a table if you were popping bubbly at $350 a cork.

We sat in a cozy li'l corner and C ordered three bottles of the good stuff. Cristal is a li'l overrated to me, 'cause the shit's nasty, but I'll drink and order it if a nigga's buying it.

After a couple of glasses, I got up to go to the ladies' room. As I walked through the crowed little club, I felt someone grab my hand. It was Smitty, with a devilish smile. I snatched my hand away from him and proceeded to the bathroom. My heart started racing. I felt nothing but pure hatred toward that boy.

I took my time in the restroom, hoping he would go away. At the same time, I had to get it together and walk back out there before C-God started to wonder where I was.

"Yo, come here!" Smitty said as he grabbed me again when I walked back passed him. This time his grip was much stronger around my wrist.

"Get off of me!" I screamed, trying to yank away from him, but his grip just got tighter as he pulled me closer.

Smitty put his hand on my ass. "You stuck-up li'l bitch, why you acting like that? I just wanted to say what's up to you. It ain't like I ain't already had the pussy. Stupid li'l bitch. Matter of fact, how's the pussy doing since I beat it up?"

"Get the fuck off of me, you fucking rapist," I screamed. I could tell I embarrassed him with that, 'cause his friends started to laugh.

Then one of them said, "Yo, son, you took the ass?"

"Nah, this bitch just think her shit is gold, and she mad 'cause a nigga ain't pay for that puss. Shit, she bleeds once a month like any other ho."

"Let me go," I shouted once again.

The next thing I knew, Smitty was knocked the fuck out, while C-God and Mike commenced to stomp Timb prints all over that nigga. His boys just stood there and watched, until security came and broke it up. Since the club catered to the big money spenders, the bouncers bounced Smitty's ass right up outta there, and we went back to our table to finish our drinks.

My mother's party was packed. Everybody from the neighborhood came out to show love.

I watched Keisha and Tucker out on the dance floor. They always seemed so happy. Tucker reminded me of my father, because he treated Keisha just as good as my dad treated my mom. I remembered when I was a little girl, watching the two of them together in their own little world. It used to make me sick. She'd always had him sprung, and he'd always had her attention.

Mommy did look good as ever. She was rocking a leather skirt and top. No doubt about it, I got my body and looks from my momma. She had it going on with her light-skinned complexion, short honey-blonde-streaked haircut, beautiful almond-shaped eyes, and high cheekbones. Tiara Wright was her name, and Daddy had been hooked on her since she was in high school.

"Happy birthday, Ma," I said.

"Thank you, baby. I'm so glad you're here. Do you see what your father's done? Girl, I swear I knew nothing about this party. He had me thinking we were going out to eat," she said, smiling from ear to ear.

I didn't have time to get her a gift. Besides, what do you get a woman that has everything? Dad owned six laundromats and brought his money home to her.

My father was still pretty upset with me, so neither one of us had much to say to each other. Sarcastically, he made a few comments before asking me where my boyfriend was. I didn't bother to answer him, because I knew he wasn't really concerned. It was just his way of saying that if he was a real man, he would've showed his face out of respect for not only my parents, but for me. Maybe my dad did know something I didn't, but I loved C-God, and I knew he wouldn't play me.

KEISHA

"Baby, don't go out and do something stupid. You know I need you, but most of all, your son needs you." Those were the words that ended the argument between Tucker and me; before he stormed out of here wearing a bulletproof vest and carrying a gun. He was convinced that C-God was still fucking with Epiphany, but I knew Epiphany was through with that troublemaker.

I couldn't argue with my man when it came down to his life and our safety, so I respected and supported any and all drastic measures he might have to go through to keep us safe.

I'd been calling E for days, but couldn't seem to get in contact with her. I prayed she was okay. The sooner that loser C-God was out of the picture the better off we all would be.

Every day there was different drama going on in our life. I swear at first I didn't want to move out of New York, because it was my home. Honestly, I'd never been anywhere that required flying. That's right, I was just like most of the black people in the hood that had never been on a plane and thought that going to the Poconos, Atlantic City, Great Adventure, or Foxwoods Casino was a real vacation. My wedding date was not that far away, and as soon as we were married, I'd be ready to kiss this city good-bye. The time had come. I couldn't speak for the ghettos in other states (most likely they were all the same), but here in the hood, the jealous ones would always envy; especially when they knew what you came from. They didn't want to see you come up, and trust me, it wouldn't be long before they started scheming to take what you got.

The money didn't really matter to me; my family did. But in this fucked up society, you had to have both to be happy and do what you had to do just to get by. Niggas didn't want to bust their ass to get it. They wanted the easy way out. To them, that was either someone giving it to them or them taking it.

I knew Tucker wasn't no angel. He chose street pharmaceuticals over a legit way of living—that fast money. One thing was for sure: He worked hard to get where he was without robbing or stealing from the competition. Shit, I spent many nights alone, worried sick about where my man was, while he was out grinding for this comfort zone he provided for us. Now, some sheisty-ass nigga that grew up around my way (who just happened to be fucking my best friend) wanted to take that away. Oh, hell no! It wasn't happening.

EPIPHANY

Today was a good day for shopping, since that seemed to be the only thing that kept me happy. A week had passed since me and my so-called man spent some real quality time together. I mean, I understood his hustle, but he had to lay his head down sometime. My question was, where?

Lately, all he seemed to do was pull these fucking disappearing acts. Now my dad's comments about C at my mom's party the week before had me wondering what was really good. Maybe C-God didn't respect me.

Fuck it. I was too pretty for this shit, and if he didn't realize what he had, then fuck him. It was time for me to do me.

No sooner than that "I'ma do me" thought had crossed my mind, my cell phone started to ring, and guess who it was? C-God, telling me how much he'd been missing me and that he freed up his schedule that night just for me. He let it be known that his working so hard was because of me. He wanted to give me the world. Now, who can argue with that?

Shit, those words were like sweet music to my ears. All those thoughts about "doing me" were out the window. Still, I decided to go to the mall. Who knew? Maybe Vicki's Secret had some new shit in—something sexy for that night.

On my way from the mall, I noticed Tanya walking toward her car, and her belly was big. I wasn't sure whether or not I should speak; you know, with how everything went down with me and her over C, but what could it hurt? Either she spoke or she didn't. Besides, I wanted to know who knocked her funny-looking-ass up anyway!

"Hi, Tanya. How you doing? Wow, look at you," I said, congratulating her on her pregnancy.

She thanked me with an intimidated smirk on her face. She probably read right through my phoniness—like I cared. I didn't want to ask, but I assumed she was probably due any day 'cause homegirl was huge. Pregnancy didn't agree with her looks at all. It made a bad situation worse.

She seemed very happy, so good for her. I was so curious to know who her baby daddy was, but again I decided not to pry. Shit, as long as the bitch moved on, why should I care?

"Okay, well, take care and good luck," I said as I was leaving.

"Epiphany, if you're really sincere, thanks for not having any hard feelings. I know you were really feeling C-God," she said.

My heart dropped. I threw my bags down and charged at her, ready to catch a case for beating this pregnant ho's ass. She had to be lying. How the fuck could he do this to me . . . and with her?

Tanya jumped in her car, locked the door, and screamed, fumbling with her keys as I tried to kick a hole in her door. Then it dawned on me: The motherfucker never told her about us, nor did he stop seeing her.

I calmed down and stopped to hear what she was yelling from inside the car, but she pulled off.

I was furious, and I knew she was gonna get to him before I did. Lord only knew I had to calm down because I wanted to murder the bastard.

Still sitting in my parked car in front of the mall, I called Keisha, and the minute I started to tell her, tears flooded my eyes. For some reason, however, I wasn't getting the support I was expecting from my so-called best friend. She was cold and distant.

"Listen, before you continue," Keisha interrupted, "I need to know if you knew anything about your li'l boy-friend having serious beef with Tucker."

"What? How could you ask me something like that? Of course I didn't know, and that's what I'm trying to tell you. I obviously didn't know a lot about that moth-erfucker." Not even caring about what went down with C and Tucker, I went on about what he did to me.

Days went by without me answering my phone. I just wanted to shut the world out, and all I could do was feel sorry for myself. Why me? When was my chance at happiness gonna come? Shit, I did everything he wanted me to. I never cheated. I gave him the pussy whenever he wanted it. I went out and got drunk with him, even put up with his baby momma drama, and now Tanya was gonna be number six.

All these thoughts ran through my head as I listened to "Why Does it Hurt so Bad?" by Whitney Houston on the *Waiting to Exhale* soundtrack, over and over again. I couldn't understand why he'd want to give her a baby and not me. I was twenty times better looking than her. What did she have that I didn't?

For instance, she stayed in her mom's basement and I lived in an apartment. She leased a Honda Civic and I owned a BMW. She was more of a Filene's Basement, T.J. Maxx, and Marshall's type of shopper, while I was Bloomingdale's, Saks, and Nordstrom. Now, that was a big fucking difference. The more I compared myself to Tanya, the more frustrated I became. It felt like I was putting a puzzle together but didn't have all the pieces.

SHANA

I finally moved into my first apartment. It was a small one-bedroom in a basement, but it was mine. I still had a few things at my mom's that I needed to get.

While packing my stuff, I ran across several unopened letters from K.C. I didn't even know he had written to me since he'd been locked up. The first letter said:

Sha,
By the time this letter reaches you I hope it finds you and your family in the best of health.

As for myself, I'm doing the best I can considering my circumstances. Listen, I know I'm facing a lot of time in here because the man has got me on some bogus conspiracy charges, but I am innocent and I'm gonna fight these bastards for my life. I have a lot of time to think in here, and I could not let another day go by without writing to tell you how much I love you, and I apologize for not treating you like the Nubian Queen that you are.

You stuck by me during all the bullshit, and I'll always love you for that. I hope you can find it in your heart to forgive me. A nigga needs you to drop me a line or come see me. I'll be waiting.

Love always,
Kalub Cright

Something melted inside of me. My insides got all hot and shit, because deep down inside I had mad love for him. As hard as K.C. tried not to show it when he was out on the streets, I knew he loved me too. I had to see him and drop a few dollars on his books. By the time I got to the last letter, his words were slightly different:

> Sha,
> Yo, shorty, you really shitting on a muthafucka. I guess you ain't really give a fuck about me 'cause now a nigga fucked up and I can't even get a few words on some fucking paper from you. Yo, that shit hurts, word up. I took care of your bum-ass when your people ain't do shit. I ain't never asked you for nothin'. It's all good though. A nigga see what's really good. U take care. Breathe easy, baby girl.
> ONE

I wasn't even gonna trip 'cause these letters were dated back three and four months before. He was only speaking out of anger 'cause a nigga thought I shitted on him.

After making a call to the house where at least 75 percent of our black men reside, Riker's Island, I was told that he was transferred Upstate. It took me a week to find out his exact location and information, but I had to see him.

EPIPHANY

Listening to him beg and plead on my answering machine several times a day didn't help much. It only made me weaker and more eager to hear what he had to say, even though it wouldn't matter now after all the bullshit that went down. I wanted to talk to him and needed to hear what he had to say, his side of the story. As much as I tried to fight the feeling of missing his no-good-ass, I couldn't. It's a difficult situation when your heart won't feel what your mind needs it to.

It had been twenty-four hours since my phone stopped ringing, and the thought of C just giving up on me made my heart hurt. I checked my caller ID to make sure I didn't sleep through any of his calls, even though I really hadn't slept much. I just needed to make sure. I would rewind and replay every message over and over again, until I finally stopped fighting it and called him up.

The first ring had my heart pounding. Second ring, it pounded even harder. Third ring and then his voice-mail, my heart dropped into the bottom of my stomach. I hung up the phone wishing I had never called him at all. Damn, I should've just picked up the phone. Maybe he was with Tanya, I thought, feeling partly to blame for him saying fuck it.

Ring!

Oh, shit. That was my phone. I jumped up and ran to the caller ID to see if it was him, 'cause that would determine if I would answer or not. It was him. My heart started pounding again.

I picked up, speaking in a tone that showed no pain. "Hello?"

"Epiphany?" he hesitated, unsure that it was me.

"Hey," I said.

"Did you just call me?" he asked.

That's some bullshit. He put the ball in my court to start off the conversation. I threw it right back in his.

"Well, I was out of town a couple of days, and I got your messages, so I was just returning your call." Yeah, I lied about being out of town, but I wasn't about to let this nigga know that I was in the house all week, fucked up and losing sleep over him. "So, what's up, C-God? What you gotta say?" I said, giving him and myself the benefit of the doubt to at least hear what he had to say.

"I need to talk to you face to face," he said. Face to face was too easy. He was probably thinking if I saw him I'd get weak. That's what that was all about, and I wasn't going for it.

"Listen C, whatever you have to say can be said over the phone, 'cause I don't wanna see you. Oh, and no more lies, please." I threw that in to let him know that I was fed up with his bullshit.

After an hour of listening to what he had to say, I learned that he just found out Tanya was pregnant, and it happened before we grew close. He also said he wasn't sure if it was even his. Although she said it was, he heard she was fucking with someone else. C also said he was gonna tell me once he knew whether or not he was the kid's daddy. He said I needed to know she meant nothing to him.

I was somewhat convinced, but I didn't want to make getting back with me too easy, so I brought up his beef with Tucker.

"Yo, that was just a small beef over some nonsense. That shit has been squashed. So when can I see you?"

"Whenever you want to," I replied eagerly, as excitement started to take away the pain.

SHANA

K.C. and I kicked it, and everything was all good. Seeing him made me realize how much I really loved that nigga, and he needed me to be in his corner. Since he'd been locked up, his peoples had been shitting on him, so he'd been on some fuck-the-world type shit. He said I was his first visit since he was shipped Upstate, and seeing me made a nigga feel like he had something to fight for.

He was waiting on an appeal, 'cause there was some foul play on the state's part, which meant he might be coming home. But his lawyer needed ten G's to proceed with the appeal. Three visits later, collect calls, some sneakers, underclothes, lawyer's fees, and about six hundred dollars in commissary, he asked me to marry him.

K.C. always knew the right shit to say to me, but being in jail made him more sensitive, respectful, and loving. With all that in mind, I said yes. I had a lot of shit going on in my life that he knew nothing about, and I didn't need him to know. His freedom card had been revoked. He was in there, and I was out here tackling life every day, doing what I had to do to survive.

It was funny how life took its turns. When he was on the streets, he took care of me, but he also did his dirt. Now it was my turn to take care of him, not because I owed him, but because I loved him and I was a rider for mine.

I no longer needed to fuck with C-God, now that I had my own connect with his supplier. I was making twice as much as I did when I was working for him, but he served his purpose. Once he put me on, we ain't fuck around that much. It became mostly business, but we remained cool. You never burn bridges with a nigga like him. I liked them thugs, but on the real, that nigga was a li'l too self-destructive for me. He was either gonna end up dead or in jail. I didn't want to be caught up in that shit when it happened.

Chasity was on some new shit, so I stopped fucking with her altogether. That licky-licky shit wasn't my thing anyway. Them fucking chicks wasn't nothing but a headache, worse than a man. Shit, trying to keep up with that kinky threesome shit was wearing me the fuck out. Not to mention her jealousy when it came to me and C having sex and not including her. The bitch would start getting all emotional and wanna fight me. I wasn't with that. I was making moves now, and I ain't had no time for headaches.

I had rings to buy. I never put that much thought into getting married, but I knew one thing: if I wasn't paying for my own ring, it would have been a much better one. Shit, they say that diamonds are forever, and looking at how much they cost, they should be. Picking out K.C.'s band wasn't hard at all, but every ring that I liked cost three thousand dollars and up. I settled for a nice little diamond chip cluster that cost me six hundred bucks. I didn't need people asking questions about no big-ass rock on my finger.

As I was leaving the jewelry store, I ran right into Keisha. She was the last person I wanted to see. Her expression was cold, and I knew she had every reason to be salty. I hugged her and tried to play shit off, but she wasn't falling for it. She hit me with every question that she could think of. I told her I was going through a tough time and just needed my space. It wasn't personal.

I did miss Keisha. She was always a sweetheart. I knew I could have at least returned her phone calls. My problem wasn't really with her. I started to feel bad for cutting the only true friend I'd known for half my life. With all that said, I saw a look of true friendship in that girl's eyes, more that what I probably deserved.

Keisha forgave me ,and even though it was too late to be in her wedding, I was going to make it my business to at least be there. I owed our friendship that much.

EPIPHANY

There wasn't a lot of talking going on between C-God and me last night. When I opened up the door and seen my man standing there, I forgot why I was even mad at him in the first place. As a matter of fact, I was mad at myself for staying away from him so long. From the time he walked in the door up until the moment he left, there was nothing but straight fucking—I mean lovemaking—going on. His lovin' was definitely what Epiphany Janee Wright needed to get back on track.

The way he sucked my pussy took me to a world of fucking ecstasy. As my legs started to tremble, the need to feel him inside of me grew stronger. I pulled him up from my drenched pussy so I could taste it from his lips, and as usual his thick ten and a half inches of hardness knew how to find its way home. I missed being fucked so good. It was long overdue.

My pussy started to throb every time I thought about my sweet chocolate boy wonder. I gave it to him any way he wanted it and in every hole he wanted in. C had always been crazy about my head job, and that night I almost sucked the skin off it and gargled his babies before I swallowed them.

I was really feeling myself after he screamed out, "Damn, I love you!" I wanted him open off of me, so I gave him all I had to give, including my chocolate factory (meaning my butthole). For those that don't know, that shit hurt like hell until he got it all the way in. C didn't ask no questions when I got on all fours, doggy style, spread my ass cheeks apart and gave him my best "fuck me now" facial expression. Why should he, after months of me refusing to take it there? He was so gentle, and just like he said, the key is to, "relax your muscles and take deep breaths." From there on out, it was a beautiful thing. God, if loving him was wrong, I didn't want to be right. And if loving him meant keeping it from Keisha, so be it.

Speaking of Keisha, that afternoon was the first wedding rehearsal brunch, and I swore if I didn't have to be there, I wouldn't. Two wedding rehearsals for a wedding that was less then two weeks away. Who the hell needs two lessons on how to walk down a damn aisle and carry flowers?

C-God left me drained of all energy, so sleep was what I needed to recharge my batteries. Unfortunately, I had to drag myself up out of bed and into the shower 'cause Lord only knows if I was late, I wouldn't hear the end of it.

The rehearsal was longer than I anticipated and a li'l boring, but very well organized. Keisha always wanted everything perfect, especially that day. Shit, if I didn't know better, I would've thought today was the real deal 'cause my girl was on cloud nine. I wasn't mad at her, though, 'cause I'd be too if I was marrying the love of my life.

I had yet again come face to face with Malikai, who had barely said hello to me or paid me any mind, and I was looking so good. I remember the last time we all got together for the baby's christening. The nigga couldn't keep his eyes off me, and he was with a bitch. I felt a li'l awkward because we had to be partnered up side by side for a while during rehearsal, and while everyone was laughing and joking with their assigned partners, he wanted to be bitter. But for the most part, I ain't really give a fuck. My mind was on C and getting out of there to be with him.

On my way home I blasted "Love's House" with Eddie Love on WBLS. I was definitely in the mood for love. I even did his "take a deep breath and exhale" routine. Shortly after that, he took it there when he played SWV's "Weak." Damn, that was my shit back in the day. I smiled as I sang the chorus: "I get so weak in the knees I can hardly speak. I lose all control and something takes over me." I was loving this song even more now that I could relate. A nigga damn sure had me feeling weak and outta control. Shit, I was ready to propose marriage to his ass and become Mrs. Corey Hinderson.

When I got home, there were two messages flashing on my answering machine. I pressed play and began listening while I undressed. The first one was from C. I wondered why he didn't try me on my cell, until I heard him canceling our plans because of unexpected business. That answered my question: He didn't want to hear my mouth. That was why he chose to just leave a message on my home phone.

He ended his message with, "I'm sorry. Don't be mad. I'm glad you're back in my life. You know I love your pretty-ass, girl. I promise I'll make it up to you. Keep it warm. I'll call you later." With all that said, how could I possibly trip or be mad? I'd been dealing with him long enough to know that business came first.

Message number two made it rain on my whole fucking parade. At first I couldn't make out the voices because there was a lot of giggling, kissing, and moaning going on, and then loud and clear I heard the muthafucka say, "Mmmm, Tanya."

My mouth dropped as my machine went, "Beep! You have no more messages in your mailbox." I ran over to my caller ID box to check the number. I clicked back to the first call to make sure I wasn't bugging the fuck out. Both calls came from C's cell phone. I ran over to my phone book to compare the numbers, hoping that maybe it was the wrong number, even though I knew there was no way possible. Ain't it funny how fast shit changes? Just a minute before, I was on top of world, and just that quick this muthafucka done knocked me down. I couldn't understand it. Why?

How could he do this to me again, and with that bitch Tanya? I screamed. My pussy was still fresh on his breath, and here he was doing God only knows what with the next bitch. Oooh . . . I couldn't stand her, and I hated his black ass.

I played the message again just to analyze the whole shit, then I saved it to use against his ass before he could even think up a lie. I figured it out. You see, his first message about "Oh, I can't make it 'cause of some unexpected business" message was left at 7:32 p.m. By 8:05, when the next call came, he was taking care of business, all right. I must have been the last call he made, and somehow his cell phone dialed me back.

Well, tha was it. I wouldn't be falling for the okey-doke no more. If he wanted to be with that skank, fine. I was through crying. Besides, I could do much better in the looks department.

I felt sorry for their kid, 'cause Tanya wasn't much to look at and neither was he. Tears filled my eyes as I asked myself one question, *Why couldn't I be happy?*

As much as I didn't want to feel it, I couldn't help it. I was hurting inside. I dropped to my knees, once again with emptiness in my heart. Trying to hold back my tears, I did something I hadn't done since I was little. I got on my knees and asked God to please help me through this.

SHANA

I hadn't missed a visit since me and K.C. decided to work on this jailbird love affair. Especially now that I was officially his Mrs., and needless to say, when we had our first conjugal visit, we fucked like bunny rabbits. It wasn't nothing like being the first piece of pussy a nigga had in a while. We also talked about the streets, my hustle, and our future plans.

Things were looking up for him. That's right, my man might be coming home sooner than we expected. His lawyer discovered that there was some hidden evidence and foul play on the arresting police officer's part, so his request for an appeal had been granted. He also got some connects in house, so the papers were processed faster.

I saw K.C. really wasn't ready to change though. Just like most of the niggas doing time, always talking shit about how when they get out they gon' come home and do the right thing, and as soon as they get out . . . bam, right back to doing the same shit that cost them their freedom the first time. K.C. hadn't even smelled freedom's air yet and here he went. He was already asking me to help him set up C-God for fucking up this kid Smitty that he's supposedly real cool with.

Smitty got a baby by K.C.'s li'l sister, and he looked out for K.C. from time to time, hitting him off with a li'l dough for his books before I came back on the scene. I didn't want to get involved in that shit at all. Nope, I

didn't want no parts of it. That nigga C had a lot of en-
emies, but I ain't wanna be one of them. He looked out
for me, and if it wasn't for his connect, I wouldn't have
been on now, or able to keep paper on K.C.'s books like
I'd been doing.

I told him that I worked for C for a while, pushing E
pills, and how he respected my gangsta so much that
he put me on to his li'l hideout spot where he kept all
his pharmaceutical supplies and money. Even how he
threatened to kill me if I ever crossed him. Yeah I told
him everything, except for how often we used to get our
fuck on, or about Chasity, for that matter. His homo-
phobic-ass might've killed me or himself if he found out
about that. Still, I didn't wanna burn that bridge with
betrayal. C-God ain't never did me dirty, and I never
knew when I might need him again.

Although I hadn't heard from the nigga, I didn't think
there was any bad blood between us. Hopefully he
wouldn't suspect I dropped dime and come looking for
me. If he did, I hoped K.C. had my back, 'cause now and
forever my loyalty was with my man—but I would do
what I had to do to protect myself if it came down to it.

On a lighter note, that night was Keisha's bachelorette party, her last weekend as a free women. Well, shit,
she wasn't ever free, so let's just say her last weekend
with the last name Moore. She had no idea that I was
now a married woman, so I had some celebrating to do
myself, and I was ready to get my party on.

EPIPHANY

I woke up that morning feeling like the Lord was probably gonna work on me slow, because I still felt like shit. I knew if I stayed in this house it would only get worse, so instead of canceling my 10:00 a.m. appointment with Ardie, I decided to get my ass up. First things first, I had all my numbers changed, because I didn't want no parts of C-God or his lies. I had to start somewhere, and that somewhere meant avoiding his ass by any means necessary. On my way out the house, I grabbed two CDs that I knew would help ease my depression: Mary J's *My Life* and *No More Drama*, because I damn sure couldn't take any more drama in my life.

As soon as I arrived at the shop, Ardie rushed me to the back and got started on my wash as usual.

"Girl, where you been at? I ain't seen you in a month of Sundays. I know you ain't seeing a new stylist, 'cause, girl, your hair is a hot mess."

I gave into his prying and started telling him all the shit that C was putting me through. Ardie was a straight drama queen, so if anyone could give me some advice, he could. The only thing he kept saying was "What?," "Uh-uh, girl," and "Oh, no he didn't."

When he finished up with my hair, Ardie spun my chair around toward the mirror. "*Voila!* A star is born. Girl, look at you. Besides the fact that I do know how to work a miracle, you are too pretty to be going through this kind of bullshit. Now, suck it up and go find you a winner. Forget that loser, honey. Humph! Life is too short," he said, sucking his teeth. "Shoot, girl, let me tell you something. You are lucky I love me some dick, 'cause I would've been after you, Ms. Thing." I fell out laughing. "Don't laugh, girlfriend. That's a compliment," Ardie said, placing his hands on his hips.

Now it was definitely time for me to go. Ardie's words did make me feel better, but that was a little too much information for me.

My new style was looking tight. I exhaled and left there feeling like I could breathe again, work it out, and feel unfoolish about it all. That's right; JLo, Béyonce, and Ashanti put together ain't have nothing on me.

I hopped in my car and continued to blast Mary. Singing along with "Rainy Days," I decided to go see my parents.

When I pulled up to the house, my father looked like he was on his way out, and my mother's car wasn't there. He greeted me with a smile and, of course, some sarcasm. "Hello, stranger. Long time, no see." I wasn't gonna stay, but he told me to come inside.

"Where is Mommy?" I asked, still calling her Mommy like I did when I was little.

"She got a new gig working at Citibank as a financial consultant, and if nobody else knows, I know she can stash away some cash," he said, laughing. Most likely, he was referring to all the G's she done stole from his stash back in his hustle days. She used to call it the "Just in case a nigga wanna act up" fund. She never knew he knew she was stealing his cash, because he never said a word.

Wow, I wondered what made Mommy want to start working after all those years. Even though she held down every one of Daddy's laundromats, it never took her long to hire help. She liked being the boss, giving orders and collecting the dough.

Daddy always had a way of knowing when something was wrong, especially when I didn't want him to know. He looked at me and said, "Epee, what's going on with you?"

"Nothing, Daddy. I'm good," I answered back, trying to avoid direct eye contact.

"So, what do you plan to do with your life, Epee?"

"Daddy, I really don't want to get into this."

"Well, Epee, it's time we do. I'm your father, and I really don't get into your business as much as I should. I know I let you get away with a lot as a child, but you're an adult now, so it's time you start making better choices for yourself . . . first, with the niggas you choose to run around with. You know what they say: sometimes we choose our own poison, and that Hinderson boy is gonna take you out slow."

I rolled my eyes and folded my arms like I always did when I didn't get my way, which wasn't often. Today, I could tell it wasn't going to work.

"Look, Daddy, I don't see him anymore, and I know you love me, but I don't understand how the same kind of people you want me to stay away from is the same kind of person you used to be. Have you ever thought that maybe I'm attracted to that lifestyle because that's the way you made me? I want someone to take care of me financially so I don't have to work. I want to be able to get up and catch a plane to the Bahamas or cruise the islands whenever I want. I wanna do all the things you and Mommy did when you guys were neglecting my needs."

My father's facial expression changed. His face became full of hurt when I said that last part, but it was true. All those years, I never told my parents how I really felt. Since he was the one that wanted to talk, I felt it was time I told him how I was feeling.

"Epee," he said, "look, I always tried to give you everything, and if I could do it all over again, I wouldn't change that. I tell you to stay away from my kind 'cause I know shit you don't. And I also know that it's not the life I want you to have.

"Besides, shit is different since when I was in the game. In my days, if you were fine, a brother would do anything just to have you as a trophy on his arm. Now niggas don't care how fine you are no more. It's about what's upstairs. It ain't about the looks no more, because don't no man wanna take care of a woman that can't take care of herself, especially a cat out there hustling in them streets.

"They're looking for a woman that's about something, meaning going to school and getting that education, getting good jobs, and let's not forget establishing good credit. You see, they're going for the corporate type. The strong ones that'll hold 'em down, Epee. It's like an investment 'cause if they gotta do some time for doing a crime, a nigga expect his lady to hold it down until he gets out.

"Let's say he wants to buy a car, house, or whatever. He gon' look for her to sign for it because her credit's good.

"Epee, listen to me. I ain't gon' tell you nothing wrong. I've seen, done, and been through it all. I was just one of the lucky ones who had a good woman that put up with a lot of bullshit and stuck by me when I was out there doing shit to her and had no business doing it. You see, I had that mind frame that a lot of men out here have when they taking care of everything: You do what you want. A lot of the shit I did for your mother, I did it out of guilt because I was fucking up.

"I'm glad I'm still here to tell you all these things, because as long as I was out in those streets, hustling and doing fucked-up shit, I should've been locked up somewhere or dead a long time ago. That's how it usually ends up. Niggas don't care 'bout you, your family, or none of that. They'll kill you just because of your affiliation. I've seen it happen. So, trust and believe me when I tell you how lucky I am to be here. God kept me here for a reason, and I believe that reason is to make sure my baby girl is all right."

With all that my father just said, I started getting emotional when I thought that maybe that was C-God's reason for holding onto Tanya. Everything my father said made a lot of sense. She was not cute, but she had a degree, a decent job, and probably good credit, and all I had were good looks and material things. I couldn't hold it back any longer. I started to cry.

My father came closer to comfort me. It reminded me of when I was a little girl, how I used to cry and throw tantrums thinking that it would keep him from hitting the streets, because I didn't want him to leave. He would hold me tight and say, "Epee, Daddy loves you, and it's gonna be all right. Daddy'll be back."

I couldn't tell him that the nigga he loved to hate got me on this fucking emotional rollercoaster. My father squeezed me tighter and apologized for all the time I might've needed him and Mom and they weren't there. I guess now I understood that they were young, and they showed me love the best way they knew how.

KEISHA
THE BACHELORETTE PARTY

Shana insisted on picking me up. I wasn't too sure I trusted her driving, but I agreed because after I got my drink on, I didn't think I'd trust myself behind the wheel either. Lea and Simone, my two friends from school who shared the same major as me, went all out putting this li'l shindig together for me with the intention of getting me pissy drunk. I would have preferred just having a girls' night out at the club. Lord knows I hadn't been to a club in a while. But Lea wasn't having it. Her exact words were, "Girl, this is your last chance to live a little. You can go to the club anytime, but you might not ever get another chance to see some beautiful black men slinging big dicks in your face. You just remember to thank me when it's over, girl."

Shana arrived at my house a little early looking real cute. She handed me a medium-sized box wrapped in silver and white wrapping paper with a big, pretty white bow. "Here. This is for after the wedding," she said, giving me her best strip tease dance while singing "Nasty Girl" by Apolonia 6. We both started laughing, then I noticed she was wearing a nice li'l ring filled with small diamonds on her left ring finger. I grabbed her hand.

"Oooh, what's this all about?"

She smiled and said, "Oh, I ain't tell you I was married."

"No, bitch!" I screamed at her like we always did back in the day when one of us was holding out on some juicy information. Then I proceeded to ask details like who, when, and for how long?

"Congratulations, girl. Now when is K.C. coming home?" I said, chasing her around for a hug.

On the way to the hotel, I asked Shana to please be cordial to Epiphany and told her that she has to tell her how she feels one day, just not tonight. We had been friends for a long time. We'd seen each other go through some heartaches, pain, good times, embarrassments, and struggles.

"Shana, we both know that Epiphany is full of herself. She's conceited, self-centered, and self-righteous; just plain self-absorbed. She can't help it. That's just the way she is, and that's the way she's been since we've known her, so don't end a long-term friendship over something she can't change. We all got personality issues, maybe not as bad as Epiphany, but we love each other, and I know we'll always have each other's backs, so try to forgive her 'cause she knows not what she does." We both busted out in laughs. With all that said, Shana agreed and even admitted to missing her a little bit.

It was party time! A room filled with about seven of my closest friends and associates yelled out when I arrived to room 202 at the fairly new JFK Sheraton right off of 150th Avenue. The girls had a connecting two-room suite decorated with mini brown dicks hanging from streamers, chocolate dick-shaped lollipops, and a cake with a big dick on it.

"This is ridiculous," I said with a smile. "You guys done went dick crazy."

"Well, enjoy," Lea said, "'cause the best is yet to come."

I was surprised to see Epiphany there so early, and she was surprised and happy to see Shana. She ran over and gave her a big hug, and everything seemed to be fine, for now. Simone was playing deejay, and her li'l boom box packed a lot of bass. She played some of the hottest songs from way back in the days, while we all tried to remember all the old dances like the whop, cabbage patch, and the Smurf.

The party really started to jump off when the entertainment came, which was right on time. Although I couldn't speak for anybody else, I was feeling a li'l hot and a lot tipsy.

Since Lea was the host, she stood up over by the door of the connecting room and introduced three of the finest shades of chocolate men I had ever seen in my life (at least that was how the alcohol made me feel).

"Let me present Mr. Goodnight. He'll put that ass to sleep. Chocolate Ty will take you on a natural high, and oh, yes . . . last but not least, The Damager will put a hurting on the pussy."

I almost dropped my drink when he stepped out of the other room. He had a caramel complexion that could just melt in my mouth. Standing about six foot three with a baldy, his chest was covered with a fine texture of hair, and the bulge in his pants was unbelievable.

They gave Simone a tape to pop in the cassette with songs like Ginuwine's "Pony," Jodeci's "Freakin' U" remix, and R. Kelly's "Sex Me." All three of them immediately came over to me and got the party started. Chocolate Ty picked up me and the chair I was sitting in, while Mr. Goodbar—I mean Mr. Goodnight—laid down on the floor what appeared to be a clear shower curtain and then me. I closed my eyes, feeling a little nervous about what was about to happen next. Then all three of them participated in covering my body with saran wrap, whipped cream, chocolate syrup, and a variety of fruits, then one by one, starting from my toes, they licked me off. The best was saved for last.

When I opened my eyes, The Damager was on top of me. I wanted him so bad; the way he touched me made my heartbeat jump between my legs. While the other two were keeping the girls preoccupied, The Damager gently tugged on my shirt, leading me into the other room. I didn't try to stop him.

He closed and locked the door then grabbed me by my hair, stuck his long tongue in my mouth, and started caressing my body. His touch felt so good my knees started to buckle; bad enough I only stood five foot two inches against his very large frame. He picked me up and slowly, still working his tongue, walked me over to the bed. I didn't know what came over me, but I knew what was about to happen, and not one bone in my body wanted to stop it from happening.

My heart pounded as he began to undress me, and with no hesitation he stuck at least twelve inches of hard dick inside my pulsating, wet pussy and fucked me until my legs started to shake uncontrollably. Then, just as it felt like my insides were going to explode, he snatched his hardness out of me, making me feel like a dope fiend without his dope as my pussy throbbed so hard.

He made me beg for more as he whispered, "Tell me how bad you want me."

"I want you. I want you so bad," I moaned as he bit on my neck and breast.

Then he demanded I turn over on my hands and knees so he could toss my salad. After he finished licking and sucking on every inch of my ass, he inserted his dick again and pounded me out from behind, shifting all twelve inches or more up in my guts, giving me a feeling that I had never felt before in my life.

As soon as I started to cum and thought it couldn't get any better, he put his face between my legs and slowly drank my pussy's juices. It was so amazing.

When I woke up, the clock read 4:00 a.m., and the other room was quiet. The Damager had left. I had a hangover and a sore, swollen pussy. I got up to put my clothes on and noticed he left a business card with his home number on the back. It said *Next round is on me.* I thought to myself I couldn't possibly fuck him again. I was about to be a married woman.

Then the guilt started to hit me hard. I shouldn't have fucked him in the first place. What the fuck was wrong with me? I waited all these years, right before my wedding, with a bunch of my friends in the next room, to cheat on the only man I had ever slept with and loved, with a stripper who probably ran around laying pipe to every woman that booked him.

The thought of him fucking other women the way he fucked me made me feel nasty. I tossed his card right in the garbage. When I opened the door to the other room, Epiphany, Shana, and Lea were still there passed out on the couch and king-sized bed. I didn't wake them. I just tip-toed over to the bed and lay down in an open space, as if I had crashed there the whole night.

SHANA

I had a migraine from all the mixes of alcohol I drank the night before. I shouldn't have gotten so fucked up knowing I had to be at the prison at 9:00 a.m. sharp in order to be able to have our conjugal visit. I was running late. There was no way I would make it there in twenty minutes, so I decided not to even try. I went home and got in the bed, hoping to sleep off the headache I had. Five minutes into a doze, the phone rang.

"You have a collect call from K.C. Do you accept the charges?"

"Yes," I said to the operator. Before I could get a word in, this nigga just started going crazy with twenty questions.

"Why the fuck you ain't here? You fucking around on me? Who's there with you, and where the fuck you been at anyway?"

"Hold up, K.C. It's too early in the fucking morning for your bullshit. Damn, I miss one visit and you flipping out on me. I'm your wife now, not one of your li'l girlfriends, so you gon' have to start trusting me," I said, feeling like I just put him in his place.

"Yo, Sha, you the only one out there on them streets really looking out for a nigga, and for that I love you more every day, but always remember this one thing about me, I trust no one, not even my momma. You feel me? Now, check it out. I need you to make it to my next visit, which is tomorrow. You got that, Shana? Tomorrow at one o'clock. I got some shit I need to run by you about that thing we talked about. Yeah, I came up with a plan."

"All right, I'll be there."

"Cool," he said, ending the conversation without a "I miss you," "love you," or even "I can't wait to see you." Boy, I tell you, unnecessary drama. It was a bad move on my part telling K.C. about my business dealings with C-God. His only concerns were commissary money, visits, and his plans to move in on that nigga C. Was that all I was to him—the missing fucking link to help him get payback? I'd been loyal and he knew that. How could he call me and say some bullshit about trust and in the same breath ask me, someone he didn't trust, to help him commit murder?

The phone rang again. I answered it, screaming, "Yes, operator, I'll accept the charges." Thinking it was K.C. again, I was ready to give him a piece of my mind.

"Damn, baby, who made you so mad this early in the morning and got the nerve to be calling you collect?"

"Who's this?"

"Oh, so now you don't know who this is? What, you got some other chick calling you baby now?"

"Chasity, what do you want?" I said, sounding annoyed.

"I want you," she said.

"Look, ain't nothing happening. I told you the last time I saw you that it ain't going down like that no more. I ain't feeling it. Besides, I got a man now, so don't call my numbers no more." I hung up and unplugged the phone.

My migraine had just gotten worse.

KEISHA

As soon as I got home, I ran straight to the bathroom to run me some water for a nice hot bath. Besides me needing one, that was the only thing I could think of that would soothe the soreness my coochie was feeling. Tucker and the baby were still asleep, and I didn't want to wake them, at least not until I got cleaned up. After my bath, I grabbed my towel and began drying myself off.

Then I remembered the gift that Shana brought over and decided to open it. I wrapped the towel around my body, still dripping a little, snuck into the bedroom and removed the pretty wrapped box from my night table. Once I tippy-toed back into the bathroom, I closed the door and tried tearing the sturdy wrapping paper open as neatly as possible, but at the same time I was anxious to see what was inside the box. It was a beautiful sheer white negligee with embroidered satin roses on it.

I slipped it on and saw that it complemented my body's curves so nicely. I admired myself in the full-length mirror behind the bathroom door and got excited from the thought of Tucker getting excited once he saw me in it. I exotically started to twist my hips to the sound of "Drop It Like It's Hot" as it played in my head, but then I couldn't believe what I saw on my left booty cheek: a big, purple passion mark.

I freaked out. How was I going to explain this and how was I going to hide it? I looked in the medicine cabinet in search of all the high school remedies I could remember for removing a hickey. The comb didn't work, or toothpaste, and neither did the frozen spoon.

Knock, knock.

Tucker knocked on the door, and my nerves started to go crazy. I threw on my sweatpants quickly and opened the locked door.

"Hey, Keish," he said, planting his juicy lips on mine. "Why you got the door locked?"

I stalled a little before I answered, trying to think of a reason why I would lock the door when I usually didn't. With my heartbeat racing, I told him the truth.

"I was trying on a little surprise from Shana that I planned to wear for you on our wedding night. If you don't mind."

Damn, that was close, I thought, until Tucker took my hand and placed it on his morning hardness.

"You feel big poppa? I woke up hard as hell thinking about that pussy."

"Tucker, you always wake up hard. Just go to the bathroom. I gotta go check on the baby anyway."

"Come on, Keish. The baby's all right. I'm horny as hell. Let me get a li'l bit. Just lean over the sink and let me hit it from the back."

"No, T. What part of no don't you understand?" I snapped at him, but really I was angry with myself for having to tell him no.

"Oh, we about to get married and it's like that. You holding out on the goodies already. Yo, what the fuck is up with that? What time did you bring your ass in here this morning anyway? You out there fucking around with Epiphany's grimey-ass, ain't no telling," he said, getting angry with me.

"Are you accusing me of something, Tucker? Because if you are, you need to ask yourself should we even be getting married," I said, flipping my wrongdoings on him. But fuck it—men do it all the time.

"I don't know. Should I be? I mean, you was out all night, and now I can't get no pussy. You ain't never told me no before. Now all of a sudden I can't have none, so what I'm supposed to think?"

"You ain't supposed to think nothing. You supposed to just trust me," I said.

This heated discussion seemed as if it was gonna last forever, and my conscience was starting to wear me down with guilt. Over and over again in my head, one side was saying I shouldn't have done it, and the other side was saying, "Fuck it. You only live once, and at least it was good." All I knew was at that very moment, I just wished the night before had never happened, the hickey was gone, and this discussion was over.

Beep, beep, beep, beep.

Somebody upstairs must have been listening, because that's the way Tucker's cell phone rang when there was drama. He called it "the warning," biting off of the way Biggie's pager went off in the beginning of his song "Warning." That meant two things: some shit just went down, or it was about to go down.

Tucker ran out of the bathroom to catch his cell before the ringing stopped. His frustration was no longer toward me but to whoever he was on the cell with, because all I heard him yell was, "What? Where the fuck was y'all at? Man, y'all some damn asses. Where's Mali at? A'ight, yo, I'm on my way." And out the door he went without saying another word to me.

EPIPHANY

I was the last one to leave the hotel room. Since I had no one to go home to, there wasn't any rush. I ordered the deluxe breakfast from room service and went back to sleep until checkout.

I had a good time the night before, 'cause it gave me a chance to get my mind off of you-know-who and to hang out with my girls like we used to.

I couldn't believe Keisha had given up her goody-twoshoes crown that night. All that moaning she was doing in the other room made me want to form a line at the door and go next. I knew she had some bad girl up in her somewhere.

That was my girl. Shit, niggas had been doing it for years and still were. Look at C's cheating-ass, telling me he loved me and then when he left me to go and take care of so-called business, he was laying up with the next bitch, playing house and picking out baby names. I hated that lying bastard.

Speaking of the devil, I approached my street and noticed C-God's truck parked in front of my apartment. I got weak from the sight of his truck, I knew mentally I wasn't ready to see him face to face, so I just kept driving.

Once again the pain took over. Trying to fight depression, thoughts of encouragement stroked my ego. *Epiphany Janee Wright, snap out of it. You're the one in control. You're strong, tough, the one who gets what she wants and then breaks away. A certified heart-breaker . . . with a broken heart.*

No matter how hard I tried to convince myself, it wasn't working. It's so hard to get out of the situation when your heart won't do what you want it to do. It felt like I had fallen and couldn't get up.

I ended up at the mall on Sunrise Highway. Shopping always made me feel better. Unfortunately, I saw nothing I wanted, so I only purchased a bottle of a new fragrance by BCB Girls called Nature and headed back to the car. I assumed the coast would be clear by now, 'cause that nigga C ain't had no time to be staking out in front my crib like that—not for long anyway. The streets were always calling him.

As I was driving, I noticed this hooptie speeding up alongside me. At first I wasn't sure who it was, but as Smitty was passing, he pointed his finger at me as if it were a gun and he was busting off shots. My heart pounded in fear, because there was no telling what that crazy muthafucka would do.

C-GOD

"Yo, what up, Mike?"

"Yo, C, that shit was a piece of fucking cake last night. We got them niggas shook, son. Took all their shit, yo. Where you at, man? 'Cause I know you don't want the details over the phone," Mike said, thinking like a lieutenant was supposed to.

"Naw, you right. I'm out here in front of this bitch E crib. Yo, I ain't heard from her in a minute. Shorty done changed numbers on me and all that, son. I don't know what's up with her. I'm 'bout to file a missing persons report out on her ass or something," C-God said, sounding a li'l stressed.

"Yo, fuck that high-price ho, man. It's something about her I ain't feeling anyway," Mike said, girl-hating as usual.

"Nah, yo, watch your mouth, dawg. Chill with that. She a'ight. Anyway, yo, meet me on the block in twenty," C said, getting a li'l sensitive over Mike's comment about Epiphany.

He got off the phone happy to hear that niggas made out all right running up in one of Tucker's spots. He already had it in his mind that Tucker was soft from their last run-in. That nigga was about to be put out of business, he thought as he drove off to go get the details.

KEISHA

My wedding was a week away, and there had been nothing but chaos in my household. Tucker and I hadn't said too much to one another. It had been a week, and he still wanted to be mad. On top of that, one of his spots got robbed for over ninety G's and a couple of keys. I didn't think anyone was hurt, but I heard the words "murder that nigga."

At first I wasn't sure who he and Malikai were talking about when I overheard them talking in the basement. I put two and two together and came up with C-God when I heard Tucker say, "We fucked up by letting that nigga slide when he was mouthing off with that bullshit 'bout putting me out of business before. He was testing me. We should've took care of that nigga then, 'cause now he's a problem that has to be handled."

With all that said, he and Mali bounced out of town early that morning, for what or how long I didn't know. All I did know was some serious shit was about to go down, and I didn't know what that could mean for our future. It seemed like the closer he got to the exit in this game, the further the exit became.

Now, here was some more shit, more drama in our lives. I mean, I wanted my shit to blow over peacefully, no more arguing between us, but now he was caught up in some danger that had his focus, and it didn't look good. The shit that was going on with him now sure took away from my shit. We hadn't talked about it, let alone had sex, and now that the hickey was gone, where was my man? Out of town a week before our wedding. Next time I would have to be careful with what I asked for because the man upstairs damn sure took Tucker's focus off me. Only God knew what kind of drama He replaced it with.

Leaving the house, I noticed a package wrapped in gold paper in front of my door. It didn't have a return address on it, and the mailman had left already. Someone must have hand-delivered it.

Attached was a card with no name that read: *I hope you enjoy this as much as I did. Best wishes.* I wasn't sure if I should open it, especially with all that was going on. It might have been a bomb or something.

I examined it closely. First I listened to see if it was ticking. I shook it and threw it in the street, but nothing happened. Not too many people knew where we lived, so it had to be a wedding gift from one of the neighbors. They were very hospitable around there.

I took the package inside and opened it. It wasn't a bomb, of course. It was a videotape with no writing on it. I popped it in the player, but nothing happened. I hoped the machine still worked because we hadn't used the VCR since DVDs came out.

I looked in the back of the big screen and discovered the wires weren't hooked up.

Damn, look at the time. I was running late. I was supposed to be at the airport to pick up my sisters at 1:00 p.m. and it was already ten minutes to. I couldn't fool with this now. I grabbed my sleeping son from the couch and headed out the door to the airport.

Their flight had already landed by the time I parked the car and finally made it inside. I wasn't sure I would remember what they looked like, since they were no longer nine and twelve but fifteen and eighteen, teenagers now.

I spotted them at the baggage claim talking to some lady they'd probably befriended on the plane. They were so pretty and still had those same faces. I decided to slightly roll my son's stroller toward them first, since he was the surprise I had for them. I then walked up right behind him, just as they were smiling at him and talking about how cute he was in their Southern accents.

"Surprise!" I yelled out, and they both jumped on me and formed a group hug. Then my sister Kelly asked whose li'l boy that was. I laughed, of course, because I wasn't used to the country accent, and said, "He belongs to me. This is your nephew, li'l T." Not only were they surprised, but I was too when the lady they were talking to turned around.

"That's my grandson?" she asked.

I had to take a deep breath for this one. So many emotions flashed through me the moment she turned around and I realized it was my mother, or should I say the lady that birthed me. I didn't know if I should hug her or slug her. To be honest, I felt like slugging her for being absent from my life for so many years, but at the same time, part of me was happy to see her. So, I went with the hug.

We all agreed on getting a bite to eat, which was a good idea because it would give us all a chance to catch up on what had been going on in each other's lives. When I pulled up in the parking lot of Red Lobster, everyone seemed to be happy with my choice. I hadn't been here in years and had a taste for it.

Inside, the restaurant still looked the same, but the service sucked. I remembered when I was a teenager, if

a guy took you to Red Lobster, he was the shit. Nowadays it was like going to Micky D's.

Besides the bad service, we had a good time, I learned
that Loretta (my mother) lived in Atlanta now, working
as a home health aide, and had been sober for 186 days.
I watched her as she bonded with my son. Just like most
men with food, French fries was the way to his heart.

My sister Kelly attended Clark University on a full
scholarship, and my younger sister hated school, was
hanging out late, and just doing all the wrong things.

If you've been listening to me up until now, you
should know how good I felt then, because family was
so important to me. Although I still had issues that
needed to be worked out between my mom and me, I
was glad she was trying. It was better late then never,
and no matter what she did, I could never change the
fact that I was here because of her and she would always be my mother.

TUCKER

"Yo, Mali, take Corn and Peewee to that motel off Rockaway Boulevard. I gotta go take care of some things right quick. Oh, and Mali, I want you to give Epiphany a call. See how she doing. Keish said she don't fuck with that nigga no more, but get back on her good side. See what she knows. She might be just the person to lead us right to that C-God."

Peewee and Corn was from the Dirty South, the thoroughest niggas you'd ever want to meet. Those niggas would rob, beat, or kill you in broad daylight. They wasn't never scared; especially when it came to doing dirt for me and Malikai. Those li'l fellas believed in loyalty to the extreme.

I had met them about three years ago. They lived in the first apartment complex I moved to down South when I started slanging dope down there. They used to sweat us because we was from New York and locking shit down. That shit was funny, because those li'l country niggas thought 'cause we was from N.Y. we had to know all the rappers out. I would send them to the store for me—and if you know anything about certain parts of the South, where it's mostly roads, you know the stores are usually far as hell—but they never complained.

Anyway, there was this kid from the other side of town. I think his name might have been Otis or something like that. He was a li'l older, and he had my li'l men scared shitless. One day, he was fucking with 'em to the point where, I kid you not, those li'l niggas wanted to cry. Me and my man Mali peeped it. We let him have his fun and get his li'l laughs off and whatnot. Then we grabbed him up, made his li'l ass strip butt-ass naked and stand still while them li'l niggas Corn and Pee beat the shit outta him. Ever since then, them li'l dudes had been straight gangsta.

That was why I had to drive all the way the fuck to North Carolina to scoop them up. They were both on parole and wasn't s'posed to leave town, so I ain't wanted them trying to catch no planes or shit like that. I didn't even think they owned IDs anyway, but I did know they'd get shit done.

We scouted all over town, from the blocks he would be at to the fucking clubs. That nigga C-God and his whole crew was M.I.A. He must have knew we was coming for him.

SHANA

"In regards to Kalub Cright, due to a tremendous amount of foul play in this case, the court finds him not guilty of the charges brought against him on January 9, 2004. However, after completing a total of fourteen days for a parole violations, he will be released. All drug charges will be dropped. Court is adjourned."

Now, that's what's up! I thought as I jumped up and ran over to give him a hug before those rude-ass court officers pulled him away. That shit wasn't cool, but it was all good because, "My man is coming home," I sang in a little tune to them as if to say, "In your face."

His visiting hours started at three o'clock. I had just enough time to get me something to eat and then head over to Riker's Island to congratulate him on his get-out-of-jail-free card.

I was happy that he was coming home, although deep down inside I was worried about him flipping on me. I wasn't stupid. I knew a nigga in jail would tell you anything if he thought it would benefit him in some kind of way. I also knew K.C. loved me, but that wouldn't stop him from kicking my ass and fucking around with other bitches when he was in the streets. I felt fucked up for feeling that way, but I liked having control while he was behind bars; there wasn't much he could do and I knew where he was at.

From the moment he sat down to the moment the visit was over, all we discussed was the plan—his plan to set up C-God. He had it all mapped out. He even made arrangements for me to meet up with that kid Smitty the next afternoon.

I agreed to meet with his homeboy. I told him I'd give up the location of C's hideout spot where he stashed his shit, but I wasn't participating in shit, and I wasn't feeling his plan.

K.C. looked at me like I had better be glad we were where we were, or else he would've slapped the shit out of me. But I wasn't going for that bullshit no more, and I told him that.

Then, of course, he hit me with some guilt shit. "Why you gotta act like that?" He frowned.

"Like what?"

"Like you ain't happy a nigga coming home or something. What's up? You don't love me anymore?"

"Yeah, I do, and I am happy," I said.

"So, knock it off and let's just do the damn thing, Sha. I told you I ain't gon' never do nothing to hurt you. You've been holding a nigga down for real, and I ain't gon' do you dirty. Believe that. Meet with dude tomorrow, handle your business, and let's get this nigga's paper, a'ight."

"C'right, your time's up," yelled the correction officer.

Before I could respond, K.C. got up and threw his tongue down my throat then slapped me on my ass.

"Daddy'll be home soon. I love you, ma," he said as the C.O. escorted him down the hall and through the steel door.

EPIPHANY

A nauseating feeling, sharp pains in my stomach, and vomiting had me up all morning. At first I thought it might have been from that nasty-ass Chinese food I had the night before, but laying there feeling the way I was feeling made me think back to the last time me and C had sex and lots of it. I knew sooner or later one of his balls was gonna make the basket. On top of that, I wasn't no stranger to the feeling. I'd been down this road too many times, but this time seemed like the worst. Instead of lying there hoping it wasn't so, I decided to get up and go buy a pregnancy test. The sooner I confirmed it the faster I could get rid of it.

On my way out the door, you'll never guess who called me. Malikai. Ain't that funny? My first question was a dumb one. I asked him how did he get my number, and before he could answer, I already knew it was Keisha. He started kicking the game about how much he missed me, and that he not only wanted me back, but needed me back in his life.

His timing couldn't have been worse. I had enough drama in my life, so I shut him down by telling him I wasn't interested. Although I did miss him a little bit, I wasn't about to make his comeback an easy one. If his ass was serious, he'd call again.

Ever since I saw C parked in front of my apartment, I'd been parking my car on the next block over. The walking distance was a pain in my ass, especially since

I picked up this laziness. I was in and out of CVS in about five seconds flat. I then stopped at the bodega on the next corner, because I had a taste for a turkey and cheese hero with a lot of mayo. The way I was creeping, you would have thought someone had a hit out on my life or something, but I just didn't want C-God rolling up on me.

On my way back to the crib, it started to drizzle a little bit, so I decided to park in front of my apartment. It was bad enough I didn't feel like walking anyway, and I damn sure wasn't about to walk in no rain for nobody.

First thing I did when I got inside was lock the door. Second, I ran to the bathroom, squatted over the toilet, and peed in the plastic cup that came with the First Response pregnancy test. In exactly one minute, it was confirmed. I was pregnant and once again smacked in the face with the unexpected.

KEISHA

I was out all afternoon running errands, something I usually didn't get to do alone. Most of time I was lugging the baby around with me.

My family had been a big help. It felt good to have them around. The past couples of days had been a blessing, because it gave me a chance to have a heart to heart with my mom and finally hear and understand her side of the story. She explained to me what her weakness was, which at the time was my father, a man that had full control of her—until he left her. She told me she felt like giving up, and alcohol became her savior. No other man could walk in the shoes my father walked in—not the fathers of my sisters, no one except a bottle of booze.

She stayed drunk all the time, hanging out 'til the wee hours of the morning, and sometimes she ain't even come home. I never knew which one of her two alcoholic boyfriends fathered my sisters, and neither did she. They used to all get drunk together and try to figure out who looked like who.

That shit was sad, but I now understood that she had a sickness and all that mattered was that she was fighting it. I also felt her pain as far as my father was concerned, because I know I would definitely lose myself if Tucker ever left me or something tragic happened.

Speaking of Tucker, he was back in town but not staying at the house. He decided it would be best if he stayed away because there was too much heat around. I was not a happy camper, but he felt it was for our safety, so I decided not to argue with that. All I knew was he had five days, three hours, and twenty-two minutes to turn down the heat before our wedding.

Back at the house, I called ahead to have the girls meet me outside to help with the groceries. As much as they liked to get their eat on, I knew it wouldn't be a problem. When I walked in the house, my mother pulled me to the side.

"I think you should take a look at this in private. The girls hooked up the VCR to play a tape for the baby and this came on. I don't think they saw that much because I was only in the kitchen for a minute, but I made them turn it off and give it to me as soon as I seen it. After you watch it, if you feel you want to talk about it, I'm right here. You hear me? If not, that's okay, but either way, I suggest you get rid of that tape."

I didn't understand the seriousness coming from my mother. What could be on this tape that was so vital? There was only one way to find out. I unplugged the VCR in the living room and carried it up to my bedroom. My heart pounded and my hands shook as I connected the wires to the back of the television. I inserted the tape, pressed play, and there I was having the best sex I ever had in my life . . . with the stripper. I jumped up and stopped the tape in disbelief.

What the fuck? This can't be?

All kinds of thoughts were going through my head. I ejected the tape and put it in the small lock box I kept in my panties drawer. I started to tremble all over as I paced back and forth, wrecking my brain, trying to figure out who could hate me that much to do something like this and drop it off on my doorstep in hopes that . . . what? Tucker and I would watch this shit together?

The funny thing was, I couldn't think of any one of the girls there that night that would want to destroy my happiness. Even though Lea kept on insisting we have some dick in our face for entertainment, what would she have to gain? She only dated Spanish guys and had a man, so I didn't think she'd do this. Epiphany and Shana, they wouldn't, so that was not even a question. The stripper guy didn't even know where I lived at. Simone and I were cool, and doing something like that wasn't even her style. Now, Tawanna and Dana, those two were suspect, 'cause I didn't know too much about them, nor had I known them long.

No matter how many excuses I tried to come up with for my so-called friends, what it all boiled down to was somebody there in that room that night wanted to break up my happy home, and I was gonna find out who.

"Who is it?" I said, responding to a knock at the door.

"Is everything okay?" my mother said, talking quietly through the door.

"It will be if you can look after the baby for me just a little while longer, because I need to be alone for a while." She agreed. Out of embarrassment and all the mixed emotions beating me in my head, I stayed locked in my room for the rest of the night.

SHANA

Chasity had been calling me all morning with straight drama. Who knew this chick would have turned out to be a psycho bitch? I didn't even have caller ID so I could screen my calls. I decided not to answer the phone anymore. I just hoped K.C. didn't try to call me, 'cause he'd be trippin'. I had already spoken to his boy Smitty and confirmed our meeting. We decided to hook up at the food court in Queens Center Mall, somewhere crowded and noisy.

When I got to the mall, the nigga wasn't there. He told me that he would be wearing a Philly 76ers Allen Iverson jersey, blue jeans, and some all-white Air Force Ones. I ordered some KFC and waited. Twenty minutes later, this nigga had the nerve to come strolling in to the food court with bags in his hand. I couldn't believe I was here to do his ass a favor and he had me waiting while he shopped. That was some bullshit, I didn't even know his ass, and already I wasn't feeling him.

I raised my hand to catch his attention. He walked over to the table on some real hard shit, like he had just won an award for thug of the year. I wanted to laugh, 'cause if it was that serious, we wouldn't be there now trying to plot his payback for C-God whipping his ass.

"Yo, what up, ma?" he said as he sat down.

"What up?" I responded back.

"Yo, ma, you look mad familiar. I seen you before?" he asked, staring me in the face.

"Yeah, that's possible. You're from my projects."

"Oh, word," he said, acting like he didn't know.

"Listen, what's really good?" I said, trying to cut all the small talk and get down to the topic at hand.

"Yo, I wanna murder the nigga C-God. Him and that pussy-ass nigga Mike that roll with him," he said in a hostile tone.

"Well, K.C. ain't say all that. He just said y'all was gonna rob him."

"Come on, ma. You from the hood, so I know you ain't no dummy. How the fuck you gon' rob a nigga like him and not split his wig, unless you ready to die? You feel what I'm saying, ma?"

"Yeah, I feel you, but if you don't mind me asking, what is y'all beef over?"

"Man, some bitch I fucked got that nigga open off her ass or something. So I'm out chilling by myself and shit at this little spot, you know what I'm saying, and I sees the bitch, right? So I said hi to her. Next thing I know, that punk-ass nigga and his boy done snuff me out and shit for speaking to the ho.

"Yo, all I got to say is them niggas is lucky I wasn't strapped that night and ain't seen them since, 'cause that's my word, niggas would've been a memory by now. That bitch too. Matter of fact, I rolled up on her ass a while back, wishing I had the gat." He started to get real hype as he spoke.

"Who's the girl?" I said, not really caring, just being nosey.

"Some bitch, man. I can't even remember the bitch's name. She a light-skin chick. She drive a fucking silver three-twenty-five."

"Epiphany!" I blurted out. Actually, I wasn't surprised at all. I should've put that shit together a long time ago, when he first said some girl who was out with C, but then again, everybody knew that nigga C-God be running around with different chicks.

"Yeah. How you know her?" Smitty sounded really curious.

"Let's just say she's like my family, and if you want me to give you the info you need, you gotta leave her out of it."

"Man, fuck that ho," he said like he had to put some thought into to it. "A'ight, a'ight, I ain't gon' fuck with her."

I knew most of the time E got on my nerves, but Keish was right when she said Epiphany was the way she was and had been ever since we'd known her. I wasn't trying to go out like that, letting something happen to her that I could prevent.

To make a long story short, I gave up the location to C's Long Island apartment in West Hempstead. The only thing about his spot was you gotta be buzzed in to get inside. To my knowledge, only Mike knew about that spot. Oh, and of course me. I also knew where Mike's baby momma lived at in Brooklyn, right off of Atlantic Avenue on, I think, Carlton Place or Fulton, one or the other. I told Smitty that Mike was always resting his head at her house.

Just as we were getting ready to go our separate ways, this psycho bitch Chasity came from out of nowhere, blowing up my spot with all her yelling and screaming.

"Oh, this is the muthafucka you left me for? This scrawny, dusty-ass li'l nigga right here?"

"Bitch, who the fuck you calling scrawny and dusty, you dyke bitch?" Smitty said, ready to scrap.

"If I'm a dyke, then your bitch is one too, 'cause she eats pussy just like I do," Chasity screamed, putting me on blast and embarrassing the shit out of me.

"Yo, ma, you get down like that?" Smitty asked me.

"Hell, no. She's just mad 'cause I don't."

All I could do was deny every word that came out of her mouth by saying, "You need to stop it. Don't be mad 'cause I ain't no fucking carpet muncher, bitch."

Boy, why did I say the B-word? She charged at me like a raging bull and started swinging. Look, I wasn't no punk bitch; I just didn't want to fight the girl. What happened next, she brought on herself.

She was still running off with the mouth and trying to fight me, so Smitty grabbed her up off of me and punched her right in her mouth. She hit the floor, and we hit the door just before security came.

Smitty walked me to my car, but ended up having to drive me home because my tires were slashed and windshield was smashed. He was amused by the bullshit.

"Damn, yo, that was some crazy shit. Yo, why she acting like that? I'm saying, you sure you ain't never licked on that girl's pussy? 'Cause that bitch is fuckin' looney, yo," he said, full of laughter.

I didn't open my mouth. Besides, it was none of his fucking business, asking twenty-one questions and don't even know me. I knew he couldn't wait to tell K.C., and that was the only nigga I had to answer to.

KEISHA

I tossed and turned, trying to get some sleep. It was only 11:00 p.m. and I could not stop thinking about that tape. It also dawned on me that I hadn't spoken to Tucker all day, so I picked up the cordless and called him on his cell. The phone rang about six times then went to voice mail. As I was leaving a message, he beeped in on the other line. I clicked over.

"Hello?"

"What's up, Keish?" he said nonchalantly.

"Nothing. Where are you?"

"Come on, Keish. You know I can't discuss that over the phone," he said.

"Well, I want you to come home tonight. I need you," I said.

"Listen, Keish. We already talked about this shit. I told you what's going on, and you guys don't need to be around it."

"Yeah, yeah, yeah. So how are we supposed to be getting married in four days if you won't even come home?" I said, rudely interrupting what he was saying.

"We won't be if you don't let me handle my business. Night. I gotta go." *Click.* He hung up on me.

I dialed him back, but my call went straight to voice mail this time. I waited for about five seconds and dialed him again and got the same results—his voice mail. This was not good. How could something that had been so good for more than five years turn bad in two weeks?

I got up from the bed and went over to my panty drawer, where I had stashed the tape. Maybe there was something on it besides me that might help me figure out who was behind it.

Within the first two minutes, a weakness fell over me as I watched the tape. I tried to ignore that pounding feeling, along with the wetness I felt between my legs, but I couldn't fight it any longer. I masturbated to the fast and slow strokes he laid upon me that night, the biting, the sucking, the licking, and kissing. That night I experienced pure ecstasy, coming close but not close enough to the phenomenal feeling of pleasure he had given me. Compared to his, my touch was a tease. I wanted more. I wanted him, but I couldn't. I couldn't do it again.

"Damn, I should've stuck to dirty chats on the Internet."

That morning, I awoke to wet kisses from my little man, while my big one watched, before he kissed me. *Maybe it was all dream*, I thought, actually hoping it was, until I sat up in the bed and noticed that the VCR light was still on and the TV screen was fuzzy. I jumped up in a panic and turned both of them off.

"Well, good morning to you too," Tucker said.

"Good morning," I replied, remembering him abruptly hanging up on me and turning off his phone last night. Before I could address it, he did, with an apology and flowers he had sitting on the nightstand. He said he needed me to understand that he was dealing with a life or death situation, and in the game, just surviving alone was an everyday struggle.

"I don't always tell you how serious shit is because I don't want you to worry any more than you already do. Just know, no matter what happens, nothing will ever change how much I love you, and hopefully my business will be straight in the next forty-eight hours so we can move on to the happy times."

With all that said, he kissed me and the baby and was gone again. At least he left me with the reassurance I needed to help get rid of all those tainted thoughts from last night: the tape and the memories.

EPIPHANY

Malikai had proven how persistent he could be. All week he'd been calling me to say hi, check on me, or just for small talk. Sometimes small talk was helpful. Last night, we'd spent about three hours on the phone reminiscing on some of the good times. I'd actually forgotten we shared so many. We got along really good, come to think about it. Talking to him made me realize I missed him more than just a little. I even agreed to let him come over, but now I was not so sure that was a good idea, because this pregnancy hadn't been agreeing with me at all.

I was sick all the time. I hadn't been able to hold any food down, so I just stopped eating. I had gone to the clinic the other day to put an end to this misery, but they told me that I needed to be at least six weeks, and I was only four.

I knew that if this was Mali's baby, things would be a lot different; especially since this would have been his first kid. We probably would have had a double wedding—Keisha and Tucker and me and him. That would've been fly. *Shit, I should just give him some pussy,* I thought, *wait two weeks, and then tell him I'm pregnant by him. Just my luck I'd have a li'l tar baby, black as hell, looking just like C-God. Nah, that wouldn't work.*

I really needed to talk to someone about what I was going through. Usually, Keisha would be the one I confided in, but ever since that incident between C and Tucker, I couldn't go and tell her I was pregnant by her man's enemy. She wouldn't understand. What kind of friend was I? If I was a good friend, I wouldn't be in this situation right now.

My hormones had me feeling real emotional and down on myself. I hated the person I was. I hated the fact that my friends had become so distant. How did we go from talking every day to only on special occasions? Oh my God, I was starting to sound like Keisha now. I hated that. I also hated not having a man to love me like I needed to be loved, but more than anything, I hated C-God's trifling-ass and this baby. That last thought of hate did it for me. I busted out into an uncontrollable cry.

The doorbell rang. I wasn't expecting Malikai for another half hour. Damn, I fucked up when I told him he didn't have to call before he came.

"Just a minute." I ran to the bathroom to fix my face, but with puffy red eyes, there wasn't much I could do to hide the fact that I had been crying.

My doorbell rang again, only this time it was more of an impatient, hurry-up-and-open-the-door ring. I ran to the door, yelling, "Okay, I'm coming."

When I opened it, it wasn't Malikai. I tried to close it back quickly, but it was too late. C-God forced his way in.

"Yo, what the fuck is up with you? You got a nigga coming by your fucking crib every day and shit looking for you. I don't do that shit for no bitch, but yet a nigga doing that shit for you. What the fuck? You thought you was gon' just play me like that? Why the fuck you change your number, huh? What, you fucking with some crab-ass nigga now or something? I should fuck you up!"

C started to get real angry when I refused to answer him. He started calling me every bitch and ho word you could possibly think of. I didn't want to show any signs of weakness, but I couldn't help it as the tears started to roll down my face again.

C-God really started to scare me with his threats. He said if he caught me fucking with anybody, he was gonna kill 'em and cut my face up bad. That threat caught my attention fast.

I looked up at him, and I could tell he was high. I could always tell, because his nose would sweat and get so wide it was scary. I had to get him out of my house, because if Mali came while he was there, ain't no telling what might have gone down. I walked over to my answering machine and played the message I had been saving for him to hear.

"Our shit is over and done with, C-God. You're busted. There's no need to explain anything, the message explained it all for you. With Tanya is obviously where you wanna be, since you supposedly ain't her baby's daddy, but yet you're still fucking her.

"You know what, though? It's cool. Y'all can have each other. I have nothing else to say, so if you'd excuse me, I got shit to do," I said, hoping he'd just leave without making the situation worse.

"Yo, E, don't give me that you-the-victim bullshit. It ain't like you ain't know shit. You wanted me to beat on that pussy from day one, and you knew I was fucking with ol' girl then. Now all of sudden you wanna act like the Virgin Mary and shit, like you got fucking morals now. Bitch, please!

"You right about one thing, though. Tanya's pussy is where I wanna be. You know why? 'Cause she got a fucking brain. All you wanna do is spend a nigga's dough and look cute all fucking day, but it's all good.

You know what? Fuck you, Epiphany." On his way out the door, he grabbed something from my hallway table. "I'm going home to wifey and my new son now. Have a nice life, bitch."

I didn't know what he took, and at that point I didn't care. I slammed the door and locked both locks, relieved that he left, 'cause he was about to find out that I was the wrong bitch to fuck with. Still, my feelings were hurt from all the mean shit he said. I lay on the couch and continued to cry as his painful words repeated over in my head.

Minutes later, my doorbell rang again, but this time I got up and ran to my closet for my nine. I wanted to kill that muthafucka.

My daddy didn't raise a soft bitch; he taught me how to shoot. When I was eighteen, he started me off with a .22, but he said those small-ass guns were only made to wound a nigga, slow 'em down but not kill 'em. Then when I turned twenty-one, he gave me my nine, something that packed a punch, and it would kill a nigga. So, if that nigga thought he was gon' come up in here again talking shit to me like I was some weak-ass bitch, then I was gonna have to show him a real bitch.

I rushed to the front door in a rage. This time, instead of just opening it, I peeked out the window first and saw Malikai walking back toward his truck.

KEISHA

It was just one of those days. Tucker called that morning and dropped a bomb on me.

"Keish, look, this ain't got shit to do with us, so don't even think that, all right? It's just bad timing right now, that's all. Too much shit is going on for me to even focus on getting married, so just call everybody and tell 'em that the shit ain't canceled, just postponed until further notice."

What kind of shit is that, three days before? How the hell . . .? I mean, what did he expect me to tell them? "We're still getting married, I just don't know when." Unbelievable! First he couldn't stay home 'cause it was too dangerous, and now he was postponing the wedding. What next? Leaving me for another woman?

This was just too much for me. I tell you, when it rains it pours. I needed some serious pampering—a nice massage, manicure, pedicure, facial, and waxing. That's what we did, the four of us. My mom and sisters seemed to enjoy it the most, because it was their first time. Me, I was a regular.

The massage was good, but it didn't change the fact that I was still upset, and on top of all that, I was horny as hell. The masseur's big, strong hands and Kenny G's "Songbird" playing softly in the background gave me a chill up my spine. I didn't know what was wrong with me lately, except for the fact that I hadn't had sex since . . . well, you know.

I was past that now. I needed some dick from my man—the man who was supposed to become my husband in three days. Now sex with Tucker seemed too far-fetched. Ever since I told him no, he hadn't touched me. I knew he had shit going on, but that had never kept him from wanting it before.

I had tried to get a quickie when he came by to check on us the last time. I even offered to meet him at a hotel, and the answer was no. So, if this was his idea of payback, he got me.

I opened up my wallet and pulled out my credit card to pay for our day at the spa. There it was, temptation staring me in the face once again—The Damager's card, the card that I should've left in the garbage but didn't. I'd forgotten all about it, but this time, as soon as I got home I was gonna tear it up and throw it away.

I tried to get rid of it; I swear. I actually thought I could, especially since the tape was so easy to destroy and discard . . . after watching it a couple of times. I needed to do the right thing for all the right reasons, I kept telling myself. I was getting married one day. Tucker was just going through some drama that had nothing to do with us. How could I even think about another man? Where was my loyalty?

My conscience was telling me to do the right thing . . . but my hormones were more influential. I started thinking about the way Tucker had been acting toward me lately, how he hung up on me, his conversations were always short now, he practically lived in a hotel, and all of a sudden he postponed our wedding. I stared at The Damager's card as I thought about Tucker's behavior. I couldn't destroy it. The devil was definitely working overtime. Using every ounce of will in me to fight the temptation, I just couldn't. My body craved him and another round of his sexual pleasure one last time. Only this time, I would do it right. Wouldn't be no tapes being made.

I waited for The Damager in the lobby of the motel. I had already paid for the room under the name Lisa Smith. That should explain what type of motel it was: no ID required, check in, do what you gotta do, and check out, no questions asked. When he walked in and spotted me, he smiled as he headed toward me. My heart started to pound as it usually did whenever I was nervous or doing wrong. In this case I was guilty of both. I thought maybe my memory of him would have been a little off, because looks can be deceiving under the influence of alcohol. Thank God, not in his case. This brother was gorgeous, better looking than I remembered.

"Hi. Kelly, is it?" he said, looking down at me with that Colgate smile of his.

"Yes," I said, smiling back at him and wondering why I gave him my sister's name.

"You're beautiful. And by the way, my name is Julius," he said.

"Okay, but if you don't mind, I'd rather call you Damager."

Julius, what kind of name is that? I thought. Besides, the name Damager was more suitable for the situation. My being here could cause a lot of damage to my relationship if Tucker ever found out. If you asked me there was really no need for us to get personal. I just wanted some dick and then we could forever go our separate ways.

I told him that I would also prefer no conversation. The less we knew about each other the better, and just so we could keep this on a business basis, I offered him two hundred dollars.

He looked at me and said, "You can't be serious. Look, I don't know much about you and can't say that I want to, but I do know you're getting married, and believe me when I tell you that I'm not trying to stop that from happening. Yes, I think you're attractive, but it is not that serious, so you need to relax with all the do's and the don'ts, baby girl. I assume we're both adults, correct?" I nodded.

"So, let's handle our business like adults and have a good time. And put your money away. Last time was a service. This time I want to make you feel good for free. Did you read what I wrote on the back of my card?" I nodded again. "So let's just get our fuck on . . . no strings attached."

Round two: It was on and poppin'!

SHANA

The past weekend's conjugal visit was definitely what was up. K.C. was so into me. We discussed everything from his release in six days to building our future together, and even one day having some kids. There was no talk about the plan or any other criminal activity. He didn't even mention my meeting with Smitty. And speaking of that nigga, I was guessing maybe he'd chilled on running back and reporting the recent beatdown of Chasity. Well, at least I hoped he had. I knew he didn't forget about it, because he enjoyed that shit too much.

Maybe Smitty was a real nigga and he wouldn't snitch me out. All I needed was for K.C. to hear that I was pussy-bumping it for a while. He hated gay people. When he was growing up, before his moms died from a drug overdose, she was one of them hard-boy type lesbians, and she was very open about it. Kids used to tease him, making jokes, calling his moms names like she-man, shim, and dyke. So he didn't want that nowhere around him. He didn't play that. Smitty couldn't have said anything about it, 'cause even though I was the only one out there keeping his bread buttered right now, K.C. wouldn't even care. He'd probably fuck me up first and then tell me to go fuck myself.

Speaking of dykes, I hadn't heard from that bitch Chasity since she got knocked the fuck out, and I wanted to keep it like that. I needed for her psycho ass to stay as far away from me as possible, and just to make sure of that, I wouldn't even be going up in Honey's anymore. I put these two girls that I'm cool with on to help me out, push my supply and get that li'l side dough outside of shaking they asses.

Raina and Silk, they was both some thorough-ass Brooklyn chicks. They didn't take no shit from them females or the niggas up in Honey's. When I met them we just clicked for some reason. Another thing I liked about them was that weed was their choice of get-high, so there shouldn't be no shorts, no getting high off the supply-type shit going on 'cause that was bad for business.

I told them about the incident I'd had with that crazy bitch Chasity, and they were ready to beat her ass for me just on GP.

"Now, that's what's up, but nah, it's cool. Don't even fuck with her," I told them. I didn't want to take it to the extreme unless I had to. In a way, shit worked out for the best, 'cause I needed some rest. Besides, my man was coming home.

EPIPHANY

I was glad Mali was there with me. I told him that I was going through a stressful time. He could tell I'd been crying, and the last thing I needed him to think was that a nigga made me cry, but his company made me feel a lot better. I didn't want to get into details, but I touched on my situation with C-God and Tanya just a little. Mali said he knew Tanya. Don't ask me how, but I wouldn't have been surprised if the bitch had been around the block a few times, you know what I mean?

He was interested in what I had to say about C, until I asked about their beef. I guess it was too soon for him to trust me again, 'cause after I asked him about that, he told me that shit was cool and he ain't wanna talk about the nigga no more. Before he used to tell me everything—well, I won't say everything, but a lot. Now he was on some hush-hush bullshit, which was cool. I knew I just had to spend a li'l time with him and shit would be all good.

Besides talking, we could play a few hands of cards, order Chinese food, and watch *Love Jones*. I didn't care how many times I saw that movie, I'd never get tired of it, maybe because I wished so bad that I had a love like Nina and Darius. I think I had love for Mali when we were together. I was not sure. I thought I loved C-God, but please, now that I thought about it, maybe I didn't know shit about love.

I got up to go to the bathroom. "You all right? 'Cause your ass is looking kind of thick in them shorts, girl," Mali questioned.

"I'm fine. That's just good living, that's all." I laughed.

"Yeah, I hear that," he said.

On my way back from the bathroom, I decided to spice things up a bit. It was only six p.m., and I wasn't ready for him to leave yet. I was feeling kinda horny and wouldn't mind giving him a sample of some of this pregnant pussy (and you know what they say: it's the best). I walked over and stood in front of him, wearing some Spandex boy-cut shorts that hugged my ass nicely and a tank top. My pussy was dead smack in his face.

He looked up at me. "What's up?" He was playing stupid.

"Don't you miss this?" I asked.

"I'm here right," he said.

I sucked my teeth and sat back down on the couch. He wasn't stroking my ego the way I wanted him to. I knew he wanted me.

"Yo, you mad?" he asked, puzzled.

"Should I be?" I answered back sarcastically.

"Nah, I don't even know why you trippin', 'cause you know I missed you. What, you need to hear a nigga say it?" he said, cracking a smile. Mali always had a nice smile to go with that sweet caramel complexion of his.

His smile made me smile. "Yes."

"Okay, cool. Epiphany, I miss the shit out of you . . . and that too," he said, pointing toward what was between my legs.

We both laughed. I moved in closer, kissed his lips, and asked him to stay with me for the rest of the night.

SHANA

Smitty called me in the morning with some good news. He said K.C. was being released that evening, but he wasn't sure what time yet, and he was gonna pick him up.

"I thought he had to do a few more days. Not that I'm disappointed or anything, but how did he get out of doing those days?" I asked.

Smitty said somebody K.C. was cool with pulled some strings in the right places and got him released a couple days early.

"Somebody like who?" I asked. I didn't trust those C.O. bitches up in them jails, 'cause I heard they be letting the inmates hit it on the low and shit. "And why he ask you to pick him up?"

"Yo, 'cause we got some shit—we got some matters to discuss. That's why." He laughed. "Any further questions, ask ya man when he get there, a'ight."

"A'ight, Smitty. Bye."

"Hold up. One more thing, Sha, before I go. Let's just say he did fuck one of them C.O. bitches in jail. Why would you even trip if it got the nigga home early to be with you? You feel what I'm saying?" His grimey-ass started to laugh.

"Bye, Smitty." I ain't even responded to that shit, 'cause four or five days was nothing. Now, years, that was some different shit. Smitty was a'ight, but I could tell that nigga loved some drama.

When I got off the phone, I took a good look at the crib, and it was a mess. It was a good thing Smitty was picking him up, 'cause I had work to do.

I put on Ashanti's CD and got busy. That was the first time I listened to her whole CD, and it was hot. I must've played that song "Baby When You Call I'll Come Running" like four times in a row. By the time I finished cleaning, it looked like Mr. Clean ran up in that muthafucka. Shit, I surprised myself. That nigga had better come home and appreciate what he had 'cause he had me running around trying to be all domesti-cated and shit. I even went out and got a bucket of fried chicken and a Pepsi to feed his ass when he got home. If that ain't no wifey shit, then what is? I was that nigga's wife for real.

"Yo, open up, Sha. Where you at? I know you got a key made for a nigga to get up in this muthafucka," K.C. yelled through the locked screen door.

I rushed to the door, opened it, and jumped right up in his arms, Whitney Houston style. That's right, the same way she did when Bobby was released from jail: just happy to see a nigga and glad his ass was finally home. I feel you, Whitney.

"What up, nugga?" I said all hard and shit, 'cause I knew that tough talk turned him on.

He palmed my ass and shoved that wet, fat-ass tongue of his in my mouth. We must've swapped spit for about a good two minutes, until Smitty interrupted the flow, opening his mouth with his hating ass, talking 'bout, "Y'all niggas cut all the mushy shit out. Wait 'til a nigga leave. Damn, dawg, it ain't like you was locked up and wasn't getting no pussy, 'cause yo, Sha's ass ain't miss them conjugals."

"Yo, nigga, stop with all the hating. She ain't supposed to miss none!" K.C. said.

"Nah, dawg, that's what's up. Yo, Sha, what up with that chicken?" Smitty asked midway through what he was saying. "Oh, shit. That's New York Fried. Yo, man, they got the best chicken; that's my word.

"Anyway, as I was saying, Shana's a good girl, man. Ain't too many broads out there that's gonna hold a nigga down. When you on the streets, maybe, but let a nigga get locked up, a bitch'll be out. Sha, you a'ight with me though, word," Smitty said with chicken grease all over his lips.

"Yo, Sha's my ride or die chick for life. I ain't never gon' leave her fucked up. She good, believe that." K.C. smiled and patted me on the ass.

"A'ight, y'all, can we talk about something else?" I said. Even though assurance was all good, I didn't want to be the topic of discussion anymore.

"Yo, Sha, you got some liquor or something so we can welcome my man home the right way?" Smitty asked.

Let me find out this nigga was a freeloader, I thought. "Yeah, I got some Henny in the kitchen."

"Oh, that what's up, baby girl. Yo, go hook us up," K.C. said.

I went into the kitchen to fix them a drink. I glanced at the time on the microwave. It was only seven o'clock. *It's gonna be a long night,* I thought. When I walked back in the living room, I knew it was gon' be an even longer night 'cause these niggas done started playing Madden on the PlayStation, and you know how a nigga forget about time when they fucking with that game shit.

"Ay, yo, Sha, we got 50's new shit?" asked K.C.

"Nah," I said.

"Yo, how you from south side and you don't have that nigga's shit, man?"

Before I could respond, Smitty paused the game. "Yo, I got a bootleg copy in the car. I'ma go get it."

"Yeah, nigga, 'cause I need to hear it. That shit is hot, yo," K.C. said, getting hyped.

When Smitty came back inside, he put on 50, sparked some hydro, and we all played puff, puff, pass. I started to relax as my high took effect, and even though I was kinda heated that this nigga Smitty ain't knew when to take his ass home, eventually it became all good. An hour later and all was high—drinking, smoking, bopping our heads to the music, and of course them niggas was still playing the game.

Knock knock.

"Sha, who that?" K.C. asked.

"Who? What?" I said, not able to hear the door through the loud music.

"Somebody knocked at your door. You ain't got no niggas coming over here to check you, 'cause if so, tell them muthafuckas Daddy's home, word up."

I laughed, trying to play it off, 'cause I had no clue who the fuck was at my door. When I looked through the screen, my high was blown.

"Can I talk to you for a minute?" Chasity asked. Something was up, 'cause this bitch was too calm.

"Nah, I can't talk right now. It ain't a good time," I said, brushing her off.

"Just open the door and let me talk to you, Cream."

Damn. Now, why the bitch wanna go there? "Yo, you bugging out. Just get the fuck away from my door please." I just gave it to her bluntly, 'cause she done made me mad calling me by my stripper name.

Then the devil surfaced, and she started banging and kicking on the thin-ass aluminum door. "You stupid bitch! Don't make me fuck you up. Open the fucking door. I just wanna talk."

K.C. and Smitty came running to the door to see what the chaos was all about. Before I could think of an explanation, Smitty had my back, taking charge of the situation. He pushed me out the way and opened the door.

"What the fuck did I tell you before, huh? Stop following me, yo, you broke-down bitch. I ain't feeling you. It ain't gon' happen, so beat it, 'cause I'ma fuck around and catch a case for whipping ya ass, yo. I'm telling you. I should fuck you up right now for knocking on my girl's door and blowing my muthafuckin' high. Get outta here!" Smitty really got a good look at her this time, and then it dawned on him where he recognized her from. As a matter of fact, he remembered where he knew both of us from—Honey's.

Chasity was yelling so much that after a while I couldn't even understand what the fuck she was saying, and on top of that, she was walking away pretty fast. I guess Smitty's crazy-ass put that fear in her the last time.

"Nigga, what up with that? Keep fucking around with them crazy-ass hoes," K.C. joked.

"Nah, man, them hoes don't be crazy until I give 'em the magic stick. That's when they lose their muthafuckin' minds," Smitty said, laughing and giving K.C. a pound.

"So, how the fuck the bitch know you was here?" K.C. asked, trying to make sense of what just happened.

"Yo, she gotta be following me."

"Nigga, you been here for how long, and she just now coming?" K.C. said.

"Maybe she spotted my car. How the fuck I'm supposed to know? That bitch a nut," Smitty said.

"Yo, nigga, that's bad business, and the shit still don't make sense, 'cause if she spotted your car, how the fuck she know to come to this house and to the side door, at that? What the fuck the bitch do—eenie, meenie, miny, mo? Come on, dawg. I'ma leave that shit alone, though, 'cause you think a nigga stupid," K.C. said, becoming annoyed.

"Yo, man, it's that hydro making your ass paranoid and shit. That's all, nigga. Chill the fuck out. It ain't what you thinking," Smitty said as he started to laugh, trying to ease K.C.'s mind.

I laughed along with him, 'cause I couldn't understand why he was going through all this bullshit just to cover for me. I barely knew his ass. Shit, he could have easily just said, "Yo, your girl was fucking with that bitch, so take that shit up with her." But he didn't, and I was glad he didn't, but why didn't he?

"Yo, I'm out, son. I'ma go take care of that thing we talked about earlier," Smitty said to K.C.

"A'ight, nigga. Hit me later," K.C. said.

"Yo, Shana, come lock up," he said as he walked to the door.

I followed behind him, and on his way out the door he turned to me, cracked a devious smirk, and said, "You owe me, nigga. Big time!" And from that, I knew I was in for the bullshit.

KEISHA

Time sure does fly when you're having fun, and I was having too much fun. Julius was such a nice guy, and he made me laugh, too. I didn't want to leave, but I knew I had to, and oh my God, the sex . . . The sex was so damn good, you better believe we fucked each other like it was our last time—and it was for real this time. I did give him my cell phone number, though, just so we could keep in touch as "friends" because we had a lot in common.

For my comfort, I inspected the room to make sure there weren't any hidden video cameras or anything while Julius showered.

I didn't shower, because I didn't want to leave him alone in the room. Not to say I didn't trust him, but the video tape thing was still a mystery, therefore everyone was still a suspect.

We departed the room at the same time. After I turned in the room key, Julius walked me to my car and kissed my forehead. (You see there, I got the forehead kiss. That definitely meant it was over.)

I reached in my purse for my cell phone and noticed I had three missed calls, all from home and no messages. The first call had come nearly two hours earlier. To me that was strange. Why not leave a message?

I called home to see if every thing was okay. My sister answered on the first ring.

"Hello."

"Hey, who's this? Keely?" I asked, not able to tell the difference between the two because of their strong southern accents.

"Nah, dis ain't Keely. Dis Kelly. Girl, where you at? Big T was looking for you. I think he was mad 'cause nobody ain't know where you was. Ma told him to call you. He said he did but you ain't answer your phone."

"Is he there now?" I asked.

"I don't know. He mighter left."

"Well, where's my son?" I said, getting a little aggravated because she didn't know the answers to any of my questions.

"Oh, li'l T sleeping. You fixin' to come home soon?" she asked.

"Yeah, I'm on my way now." I hung up the phone, thinking of a good excuse to come up with.

My nerves were starting to act up. How could I go home and face him knowing I just finished letting another man fuck my pussy? Maybe I should call him, I thought. No, I wasn't gonna call him. I was gonna go to the mall and grab a couple of things for the baby. That way I could say I was depressed about the wedding, so I went shopping. Yeah, that was a good idea. Plus, he knew my piece of shit phone didn't hold a good signal in the mall.

I was confident that my excuse would work, so I rushed to the mall and hit Baby Gap. I even grabbed a few items for myself, 'cause the regular Gap was attached. After spending three hundred dollars, I was ready to go home.

When I got there, I didn't see Tucker's car. I pulled into the driveway, and guess who was waiting to greet me at the front door? Tucker.

"Hey, baby," I said, not wanting to get too close because I wasn't sure whether or not I smelled like sex or had dick on my breath. I could tell he was furious before he even opened his mouth.

"Where you been at, Keish?" he asked in a mild mannered tone as if he wasn't upset.

"What?" I replied. Might as well see the ugly come out and get it over with.

"What? Oh, now you don't understand English. Where the fuck was you at all day, Keish? You couldn't even call to check on our son or answer your motherfucking cell phone? Huh? Answer the question."

See, didn't I say it was about to get ugly? "Tucker, if you stop yelling and calm down, I'll answer your question."

"I'm listening," he said.

"I was at the mall." I hoped I didn't look like I was lying.

"Keisha, you wasn't at the mall for no six hours," he said, giving me that "I ain't buying it" look, but that was my story, and I was sticking to it.

"Look, Tucker, I've been out shopping all day, and I just wanna take a shower and go to bed. Besides, what are you doing here? I thought it wasn't safe for us if you were here," I said sarcastically.

"Just hurry up and take your shower, 'cause I got something I want you to see," Tucker said, flashing a fake smile.

You know what? I don't even wanna know, I thought as I rushed into the bathroom, relieved that he didn't push the mall issue that much. All I wanted to do was freshen up and get through the night without Tucker asking me for any coochie, because two dicks in one day ain't cool, and if I said no again, he might really get suspicious.

When I got out of the shower, I dried off, threw on some sweats, a tee, and no body perfume or nothing. I wanted to look as unattractive as possible. I wrapped my hair, threw on a scarf, and went downstairs to make sure all the doors were locked. My sisters had the spare set of keys, so no one had to worry about listening out for them when they got home from the movies that night. Then I took a peek into the guest bedroom, where my mom and the baby were knocked out asleep. The last stop was my bedroom. I opened the door, and instantly tears started to fill my eyes when I saw Tucker sitting on the edge of the bed, watching the videotape of me giving my body to another man.

C-GOD

It was a quarter after ten and I sat in my Hempstead apartment fucked up, my nose buried in a pile of coke to numb the pain after receiving a call from Reggie about Mike, his girl, their son, and his girl's moms all getting murdered not even an hour before. Reg said he just had spoke to the nigga and they was gon' get up and go shoot a game of pool up on Flatbush Ave, but when he swung by the crib to get the nigga, the door was half open. He went inside, but before he could get far, he spotted Mike's baby moms, Angie, lying dead less than four feet away from the door, with her son in her arms, both dead. Her moms caught one sitting in the chair by the window. Bullet went throw the right lens of her eyeglasses, and Mike must've been taking a shit when niggas ran up on him, 'cause he was sitting on the toilet in the bathroom, lit up with bullets holes.

"Yo, son, the TV was up mad loud, so if they screamed, the nigga probably thought that shit was coming from the fucking tube. Man, I ain't call no cops or nothing. I just broke out, 'cause yo, shit was ugly, son. Mike's gone, and whoever did it, did my man and his fam dirty."

Those words hurt me to my heart as I hung up the phone, needing a minute to make sense of what the fuck I just heard.

Mike was my li'l brother, my soldier, the head nigga in charge under me. Out of all the niggas I put on, I had love for that nigga big time. The one thing I couldn't figure out was how niggas knew where he was resting his head at in Brooklyn. Mike was too fuckin' paranoid, and at the same time too smart, to let a muthafucka follow his ass. He stayed with his guards up at all times.

My mind was boggled. I opened a bottle of Hennessey and poured a little out on my hardwood floor, reminiscing about the fun and the drama me and Mike shared together. "To my nigga, my muthafuckin' Lieutenant Ike," I said, letting go a smile as a tear trickled down my face. Niggas used to call Mike's ass Lieutenant Ike 'cause that nigga ain't have no problems with beating a bitch's ass. He ain't care where they was. If the bitch pissed him off, he was fucking her up Ike-on-Tina style, no doubt about it.

I laughed at that thought then took a swig from the bottle and said, "I got you. I'ma kill that muthafucka Tucker, his mans, and whoever hang with them faggots. That's my word, son."

I then made a call to Ness, another li'l crazy-ass nigga on some 'bout-it, 'bout-it shit. I put him on a while ago. I liked dude, but he couldn't take the place of Mike. Still, he was thorough. Besides, I knew what niggas in my camp to call when it was time to get at muthafuckas— the ones with heart, 'cause some of them was straight pussy. Like, for instance, Reggie. He was good for making runs and a couple of dollars doing the hand to hand thing on the block, and even playing chauffeur when I entertained the bitches, but when it came to his murder game, the nigga just wasn't cut out for it.

"Yo, nigga, I know you heard about Mike, right?" I asked.

"Yeah, man. That shit is fucked up, yo. What up?" said Ness.

"That muthafucka executed my man and his fam, yo."

"So, how you wanna handle shit?" Ness asked, already down for whatever.

"Yo, just tell niggas it's time to get on they grind, 'cause we need to find them niggas tonight. I don't really give a fuck how y'all handle his mans, but that nigga Tucker, I wanna deal with his ass personally, starting with his bitch and the nigga's kid. I'ma do him like they did Mike, only worse. So yo, after you kick it to the fellas, I want you to meet me over on 137th and Guy R. Brewer, a'ight. And come strapped."

"Cool. Yo, is that where that nigga rest at?"

"Nah, this bitch I used to fuck with live over there, but she cool with his peoples, so she the bitch that's gon' give up his information."

"A'ight, yo, then just hit me when you get over there," Ness said.

"What? Nah, yo, I said meet me over there. I ain't got time to be fucking calling. Listen to what the fuck I said. Tell niggas to suit the fuck up and handle they muthafuckin' business, and you bring your ass to Guy R. Brewer. You follow me? It ain't hard if you fucking listen." I ordered Ness to follow my exact directions.

"Yo, a'ight, I got you. I'm on it," Ness said, quickly hanging up the phone.

Ness was on point. He did exactly what he was told. When he arrived on 137th, he spotted me chilling in a beat up li'l white Ford Taurus that I usually used to take runs in. He parked his car behind me and walked to the passenger side and got in.

I was zoning out, listening to Biggie and 112 singing "Missing You." We sat in silence until the song was over, then I snapped back into rare form, and the plan was murder.

I made a right onto 137th Street and crept down to the middle of the block. Making a complete stop, I spotted a red Navigator parked in front of Epiphany's crib with the license plates that read LIVELIFE. Right away I knew that was Tucker's right hand man.

I was heated, because even though I had done my dirt to Epiphany, I still felt like she belonged to me, and the fact that she was fucking with that nigga made matters worse.

I started thinking back to the night that Mike, Epiphany, and me hung out, and whether I dropped the nigga off in Brooklyn at his baby moms' crib, or possibly to one of his other chicks. I couldn't remember.

Well fuck it. That's two birds with one stone. She better be ready to die with this clown-ass nigga, I thought.

"Yo, Ness, look under the seat and give me that thing."

Ness reached under the seat, pulled out a Smith and Wesson, and passed it to me. Then he checked the clip on his shit to make sure he was fully loaded.

"Yo, you ready, son?" Ness asked.

"Yeah, just hold up a minute. I got that bitch keys somewhere in this car."

"Yo, how that happen?" Ness asked.

"I was at her crib earlier, arguing with her stupid ass, so I took them shits just to be spiteful, and now look. These shits came in handy."

"Word, yo, that's what's up," Ness said, impressed.

"Got 'em, yo. Let's do this," I said. I stuck the key in the door, unlocked it, and opened it slowly.

I heard laughing and talking while Prince's "Do Me Baby" played. I was gon' do them, a'ight. Ness followed behind as I quietly crept down the small hall leading to the living room.

EPIPHANY

Great. This was what it boiled down to, me having to give Mali a lap dance off Prince just to get some. Damn, see what a girl had to do just to get a li'l dick—and I do mean little. I ain't mind, though, because just like old times, we were having fun. I had him for the whole night. Just like he was putting me to work, payback was gon' sure be a pain in his back when I got him in my bed, I thought as I turned around toward him. I froze in shock because of what—I mean who I saw standing behind Mali.

Before I could react or say anything, they shot him in the head. His blood and parts of his brains splashed all over me. I covered my face with my hand, afraid and hurting at the same time. I didn't scream. As a matter of fact, I was in complete shock. My body trembled all over. I just stood there while C-God ordered his boy to check my bedroom and the bathroom.

Peeking through my fingers, I saw Malikai's lifeless body slumped over on the couch as blood seeped from the hole in his head. I couldn't believe what was happening. The pain I was feeling for Mali was much greater than all the pain I had ever felt before in my life.

C-God started kicking my stereo system, trying to shut Prince up, while calling me every name in the book. I was a stink bitch, a trifling ho, and then a chickenhead. Every disrespectful word you can think of, I was. I just stood there thinking about how bad I wanted to kill his muthafuckin' ass.

Then he grabbed me by my hair and forced me to my knees. He had the nerve to call me a sheisty-ass bitch for fucking around on him, and I wasn't even with his ass. He went on, saying I helped Tucker and Mali kill his boy. He then put his gun to my head. Tears poured down my face as I cried like a baby. I wasn't ready to die. I tried to release the words from my mouth, but couldn't find my voice. I tried again, and this time I was able to speak. I had to if I wanted to live.

"I swear I don't know who or what you're talking about, and I didn't have nothing to do with nothing. Please don't do this C."

"Bitch, shut the fuck up!" he yelled, knocking me completely down to the floor and kicking me so hard in my pussy. He demanded to know whether or not I slept with Malikai.

"Ouch!" I cried out in agony as I placed my hands between my legs, trying to ease the pain. I turned to my side and lay in a fetal position, crying and screaming, "Please don't hurt me! Please."

Thoughts of me fucking Malikai sent C-God into a rage. He started to lose focus on the real reason he was there. "Did you fuck him? Huh, did you?" He wanted an answer right away.

"No, I swear I didn't," I cried out.

"Shut up, you fucking lying-ass, trick-ass bitch! If I ain't come in here when I did, that dead muthafucka would've been up in that ass. You wasn't up in here dropping it like it's hot for nothing. Now tell me I'm wrong. Huh? Tell me I'm wrong." C-God didn't wait for me to answer his question. He just started kicking and punching on me like he was crazy.

I lay there with my eyes shut, balled up, trying to shield myself, wishing I could just make it over to the sofa cushion where my piece was stashed, so I could kill this bitch-ass nigga.

Out of nowhere, I heard his boy say, "Damn, son, you fuckin' that ho up. She's prettier than a muthafucka too. Word. Yo, son, you should let me hit that before you kill her," Ness suggested, knowing the only way he could ever get close to even smelling my pussy was if my life depended on it.

I could tell C didn't like that proposition very much by the look on his face, and I guess Ness could too, 'cause he quickly excused himself. "Yo, I'ma be in the front if you need me, dawg, a'ight."

C-God didn't respond. I was relieved that he left, but afraid that C was gonna continue kicking my ass. I knew I had to act fast before this nigga fucked around and killed me for real.

"Yo, E, listen. If you tell me where your friend Keisha live at, I promise I won't hit you no more." I guess that was his idea of playing fair.

I took a minute to think. I thought about how important my life was to me. I didn't wanna die. I probably hadn't been the best person or friend I could've been, but I would never be able to live with myself if something happened to Keisha, my godson, or Tucker because of something I did. I just couldn't. *Oh, God, please help me out with this one!*

"I don't know where she lives," I said, tightly shutting my eyes, shielding my face with my hands and waiting to die. He grew furious, but he didn't hit me.

I knew he didn't really want to kill me, but that didn't mean that he wouldn't. It was obvious that this nigga still had feelings for me. If I was right, then hopefully my plan would work, I thought as I grabbed my stomach and screamed like I was in excruciating pain. At first he wasn't buying it.

"You think I give a fuck about your pain? My boy and his family is gone because of that dead nigga right there"—C-God pointed his gun at Mali's body—"and his punk-ass man. So either you gon' tell me what I wanna know or yo, you gon' wish we never fucking met. The choice is yours," C-God said as if he was through negotiating.

"I don't know!" I cried. "Please, baby, just listen to me. I swear I don't know. Keisha ain't spoke to me in over a month. She kicked me out of her wedding, moved, and changed her numbers because of you, because I chose loving you over my friendship with her. Then you hurt me. You hurt me bad, choosing Tanya over me.

"And the only reason I had Malikai over here was to see if I could butter him up for her information. That's the truth. I just wanted to find out where Keisha is, because I need her. She's the only one I can talk to, and I knew she would convince me to keep it. Aaahh," I moaned in an over-exaggerated tone of agony.

Clutching my stomach, I kneeled down and whispered, "I don't wanna lose our baby."

"Baby? What baby?" C-God inquired.

"Oh, God, it hurts," I cried before I told him that I was four weeks pregnant with his child. Like most niggas, his first response was, "How you know it's mines?"

"I know it's yours 'cause I ain't been with nobody but you since I started fucking with you. If you don't believe me, just look at my papers from the clinic, there in my purse over on the table. I'm four weeks. Do the math, C-God."

I was hoping I'd get the opportunity to get to the cushion, but he didn't go for my purse. He just stood there looking in my face to see if he could tell whether or not I was sincere, and I did my best to convince him, 'cause I was sincere all right; sincere about making the bastard pay. I was gonna act my ass off if it meant saving my life, and that's what I did.

C-God finally broke his silence. "So why you ain't tell me about the baby before now?"

"I just found out about it a week ago. I wanted to tell you, but I also wanted us to be together. Then you came over here calling me names and talking about Tanya being better than me, so after all that, how could I tell you? C-God, I'm so sorry to hear about Mike. I really . . . I am, even though I didn't care much for him. I would never wish bad on him, because he's your friend and I love you so much," I said as I started to boo-hoo like crazy.

It worked! *The award for best actress of the year goes to me, Epiphany Wright, for playing on a nigga's emotions,* I thought as he fell for the okey doke.

"Yo, shit is fucked up right now. I'm fucked up. Mike's gone, and I gotta make shit right for my nigga. Word . . . I got to. I didn't want to hurt you, yo. I really didn't! I just snapped when I seen that nigga up in here.

"I ain't even gon' front, ma. I got mad love for you. Now you telling me you got my baby inside you after I done put my hands on you and shit. How you think that's supposed to make me feel, huh? Damn, E, why you ain't tell me? What if you lose my seed?"

C-God was touching, but not enough. I let out another agonizing moan and cried out, "Please, I need to go to the hospital. I think I'm losing the baby."

C-God started to pace back and forth. "Okay, wait a minute. Let me think for a minute. I can't take you to the hospital. Them muthafuckas gon' think I beat you up like that and call the police, and if I call a ambulance, they gon' see this dead nigga's body lying here and call the police."

He finally said, "Fuck! A'ight, this is the plan. I'ma have the nigga Ness drop you off at the hospital," like he was doing me a favor or something. Still pacing back and forth, he said, "Damn I gotta do something with this nigga's body. I'ma dump that shit in Baisley Pond or some shit like that, then call one of my boys to come get the nigga truck and take it to the chop shop. Yeah, a'ight, that's the plan," he said, having his shit all figured out.

"Aahhhhh," I screamed again to remind him that I was still in pain and needed help.

"A'ight, ma, let me see where the fuck this nigga Ness at." Leaving the living room, he headed toward the front door. On his way, he stopped and checked out the papers that were in my purse to see if I was telling the truth about being knocked up. He looked back at me and continued toward the door.

I jumped up and limped over toward the couch. I paused for a moment and just stared at Malikai's body lying there lifeless on the couch. I wanted to check his pulse, but I didn't have time for that. Besides, I was wearing some of his brains on my clothes, so I knew he was gone.

I pulled my nine out from under the cushion and stood up straight, just as C-God came back in the room.

"Drop your fucking gun and push it over here, you dumb muthafucka. Do it now!" I screamed.

"A'ight, you got that. Just don't shoot me," he said, dropping and kicking his gun toward me.

"Don't shoot you, what? Muthafucka, you got the nerve to tell me don't shoot you. You should've thought about all that shit when you was kicking my ass." Tears poured down my stinging face as I thought about how badly he beat me. "You bastard, my daddy ain't never put his hands on me, and since you did, I can't wait to kill you.

"I just want you to know one thing: I fucking hate you. You black muthafucka, I started wishing long before tonight that I never fucked with you. Now you gon' wish the same. You took this shit too far, C-God, and you fucked with the wrong one!" I yelled as my anger took control.

C-God just stood there in silence. He knew the seriousness of the situation from my tone. He knew that it was over and I'd had enough.

I glanced at Malikai's dead body one last time, and with the hate and anger I had floating inside me, I didn't think twice before I aimed my gun toward C-God's head, closed my eyes, and squeezed the trigger. Just as I did, I could hear Ness entering the living room, but before I could open my eyes, he blasted off a bullet from his .38.

"Oooooh!" Not knowing whether my shot was a successful one, I screamed from the burning sensation I felt as the heat pierced through my chest. I cried out "Noooo!" as I was thrown to the floor from the strong impact. Instantly, I could feel the warmth of my blood leaking from the stinging opening in my chest and my eyes getting real heavy.

The pain was too much to bear.

To be continued in

SHEISTY 2

Coming January 2016

Enjoy this quick peek at

Sheisty 2
Triple Crown Collection

PROLOGUE

Epiphany

"I closed my eyes and squeezed the trigger. Not knowing whether my shot was a successful one, I felt a burning sensation pierce through my chest. "Noooooo!" I screamed as I was thrown to the floor from the strong impact. Instantly I could feel the warmth of my blood leaking from the stinging wound. My eyes started getting heavy. The pain was too much to bear.

Keisha

I opened the door to my bedroom, and right away tears started to fill my eyes as I saw Tucker sitting on the edge of the bed, watching the video tape from my bacholorette party.

Shana

I followed Smitty to the door on his way out, and before I could thank him for covering my ass, he turned to me with a devious smirk and said, "You owe me, nigga!" From his look alone I knew I was in for the bullshit.

CHAPTER ONE

"Oh, God, please noooooo," were the last words Epiphany whispered as tears fell down the sides of her face and she lost consciousness after the shooting.

C-God damn near pissed himself. His heart pounded rapidly. For a moment he thought he was shot. Fortunately for him, Epiphany's aim was way off because she had closed her eyes when she squeezed the trigger.

"Yo, man, c'mon. We gotta get the fuck up out of here!" Ness screamed.

C-God kneeled down beside Epiphany and felt remorseful. Finally he felt her pain. In any other situation he wouldn't have given a fuck, especially when it came down to his life, but this wasn't just any situation. As much as he'd tried to front on Epiphany, he really did care for her. He had no intentions of killing her. He just wanted to shake her up enough to get her to talk.

C-God looked down at the papers still clutched in his hand, confirming Epiphany's pregnancy, and he felt even more fucked up.

"Yo, fuck that bitch. Let's roll, dawg!" Ness yelled in a panic.

Finally C-God snapped out of it, grabbed both guns, and together they fled the scene doing eighty down South Jamaica's residential back streets.

"Nigga, you must've been soft on that chick, but yo, it was either you or her, nigga. Look at it that way." Ness was the type of nigga with a big-ass mouth that didn't know how to leave well enough alone. "If I ain't come up in there when I did, your shorty might've murked you, dawg, for real. But I had your back though."

C-God just sat there wearing a screw-faced look, thinking about the "what-ifs" as he listened to Ness in silence. Deep down C-God knew Epiphany would have kept shooting at him until she killed him, so yes, he felt Ness reacted the way he was supposed to, but C-God didn't want to hear him boasting about it.

Obviously the look on his face wasn't enough, because Ness didn't catch the hint. He just continued to go on and on about the incident until suddenly C snapped.

"Shut the fuck up! Damn! A nigga can't even think straight with you running the fuck off at the mouth. Just don't say shit else to me until I ask you to, and pull this muthafucka over at that payphone right there."

Ness did what he was told. He shut the fuck up and pulled over.

It was C-God's duty to live his life coldheartedly. He never cared too much about anybody except his parents. Outside of them, the rest of his family was cool, but if they crossed him, they could easily be killed for doing so. But on the real, he was all bark with no bite, only nobody knew it because they never put him to the test.

It was his older brothers that were the truth back in the day. Niggas ain't fuck with his three brothers or whoever they considered to be family. Pop, Black, Russ, and Lloyd were well known and now legendary gangstas, ranking with some of the best that ever terrorized Queens. They were ruthless, had no respect for a person's life, and killers without a cause. If they weren't feeling you for whatever reason, then they didn't give a fuck about you or your family, and in their presence you better had shown fear.

Unfortunately, living that life came back to haunt them, leading to Pop and Russ's brutal deaths and landing Lloyd in prison for life with no chance of parole. Still, C-God felt since he was the last breed of the notorious Hinderson brothers, he had something to prove. He had to own up to his family name and the reputation they paved. For some reason, his conscience was eating away at him tonight, and that wasn't supposed to happen to no Hinderson.

C-God picked up the receiver on the pay phone. Using the papers he took from Epiphany's purse and with a piece of tissue covering his fingertip, he dialed the police. He always thought with a criminal's mind. Disguising his voice in an unrecognizable high-pitched tone, he called for an ambulance in hopes that Epiphany might still be alive.

Epiphany briefly regained consciousness, oblivious to the sounds of the loud sirens as she lay still in a pool of her own blood. An ambulance and three police cars arrived at the scene shortly after the call was made. The cops entered first and took a look around, then signaled the paramedics with, "Okay, the coast is clear."

When the paramedics entered, the police suggested they tend to the girl first. Besides, from the looks of things it was obvious that Malikai was already deceased. The EMS workers immediately ran over to Epiphany and checked her vital signs.

"She's still alive," one of them shouted. "Start an IV. Her pulse is weak. This is not good. She's losing a lot of blood. Let's get a move on it fast!" Lifting Epiphany onto the stretcher, he continued, "We're losing her. Let's get her to the hospital now!"

CHAPTER TWO

Keisha stood in the bedroom doorway completely appalled. Her heart fell into the pit of her stomach and tears instantly fell down her face. As she stood there, her fiancé was watching her give herself to another man, performing and receiving sexual pleasures on camera as if her name was Janet Jackme. She froze, stuck on stupid, puzzled as to how the videotape she destroyed had managed to resurface again.

She searched for the right words to say. She wanted to say something, but what? "I'm sorry?" No, that wasn't gonna cut it. There was nothing to be said. She'd fucked up and she knew it. She felt like she had just slid down a razor blade, right into a pool of alcohol.

Tucker's face was filled with a rage that she had never seen before, a rage that put fear in Keisha's heart. She was afraid to say or do anything, so she continued to watch him watch her fuck and suck on another man in ways she had never done with him since they'd been together.

He'd never, ever thought about putting his hands on any woman, let alone Keisha fucking somebody else, until now. Fuming, he was to the point where he really wanted to hurt her. Tucker jumped up, snatched the

VCR from the top of the fifty-two-inch TV, and frisbeed it into the wall close to where Keisha was standing.

Keisha jumped out of the way and into the hallway as the VCR crashed into the wall and then hit the floor.

Water flooded his eyes, and his heart was filled with pain. This was the ultimate feeling of betrayal, but he would never give her the satisfaction of seeing him cry. No one, for that matter, would see him cry. His militant father had instilled in him as a boy that a man ain't supposed to cry. A strong man sucks it all up and keeps it moving.

By now, all types of distasteful thoughts ran through Tucker's mind, but he never said a word. He simply looked at Keisha with anger and disgust. If looks could kill, she would have suffered a painful death.

Keisha was still standing in the hall, afraid to move or say a word. She wasn't sure what to expect from this furious side of Tucker.

Keisha's mother, Loretta, and her son, li'l T, were awakened and startled when they heard the crashing sound. She jumped out of bed, grabbed the baby, and rushed from the bedroom to see what was going on. Right outside her door, she spotted Keisha near the doorway of her bedroom, crying.

"Keisha, is everything okay?" asked her concerned mother.

Keisha didn't respond. Instead, she took it as an opportunity to get out of Tucker's sight. Making a run for the bathroom, she locked herself inside and cried like a baby.

Loretta was curious as to what was going on. She assumed that maybe it was just a heated discussion about the wedding postponement. Since there wasn't any sign of domestic violence, she felt no need to get involved, so she headed back to her room.

Tucker had no sympathy for Keisha or her tears. At this point, all he felt for her was pure hatred, but he would never hurt her because of his son.

"Let me just get the fuck up out of here," he said to himself. He quickly gathered up some of his belongings and broke out in a hurry. He wasn't sure if his anger would allow him to honor the fact that she was his baby's mother.

Once the sound of Tucker's truck sped off, confirming that the coast was now clear, Loretta laid li'l T in the bed and came back out of her room. She knocked gently on the bathroom door.

"Keisha, is everything all right?" she whispered again.

Keisha wasn't all right. Her life was over. She opened the door and fell into her mother's arms for comfort.

"He's gone, and I don't think he's coming back," Keisha stuttered as she cried.

"What happened?"

"The tape. He saw the tape."

"No! Keisha, how? I thought you got rid of it."

"I did, I did. And there's no way possible that could be the same tape. Somebody had to set me up. One of the girls at my bachelorette party, posing to be my friend, set this whole thing up, and my stupid-ass fell for it. Now he's gone, and what am I gonna do, huh? How am I ever gonna get Tucker to forgive me?" she asked her mother, hoping and wishing she could give her all the right answers.

"Keisha, you know Tucker loves you. Just give him some time. He'll come around so you guys can at least talk and try to work things out. In the meantime, you need to be strong and try to keep it together, not only for you, but for that baby boy in the next room. Don't make the same mistakes that I did.

"You know what you did was wrong, but we all make mistakes. I know you love him, and he knows it too. Understand that was a pretty big bomb you dropped on him, so he's gotta be devastated and full of hurt right now. You're the mother of his son, a son that he loves more than anything in this world, and nothing will ever change that.

"Just give it some time. He'll come around. You just have to pray for the best and prepare for the worst, just in case he can't find it in his heart to forgive you. If he can't, then you just got to find a way to move on," Loretta said, stroking her daughter's head while she cried in her arms.

Keisha listened to her mother's words, but at the same time, she didn't feel like she could manage life without Tucker. She went and got her son from her mother's bed. Holding him close, she reminisced on how happy Tucker had been when she told him she was pregnant. Their son, li'l T, was the bond that she and Tucker shared. It was a bond created out of love—a bond that because of her stupidity might be the only thing she had left of Tucker.

Before shutting her puffy red eyes and getting some sleep, she made a promise to herself to find out which one of those bitches was responsible for causing this misery.

CHAPTER THREE

Epiphany's father had a terrible ringing in his left ear all evening. Old folks used to say that when you heard a ringing sound in your ear, it was the sound of death bells and someone close to you was gonna die. Jay Wright didn't believe that ol' superstitious shit, but for some reason, this night's feeling just wasn't right.

Those feelings were confirmed when he was awakened in the middle of the night by the doorbell. He jumped up out of bed and rushed down the stairs to see who it was. It had to be some bad news, 'cause nobody rang his bell at that time of morning ever since he left the drug game three years ago.

When he reached the door, he opened it slightly and peeked out to find two police officers, one black and one white, standing there. He assumed something might have happened to his brother, Ramel, who took over his position when he retired from the game.

Before he could speak, one of the officers addressed him. "Good morning, sir. I'm Officer Johnson, and this is Officer Riley. We're sorry to bother you at this time of morning, but are you Jay Wright?"

Epiphany's dad hated the police, but he kept his composure, because finding out their reason for being at his front door was more important.

"Yes, officer, I am. What's going on?"

"Mr. Wright, I'm sorry to have to be the bearer of bad news, but your daughter, Epiphany, and a young man were found shot in her apartment around midnight. The man was pronounced dead at the scene. Your daughter was severely wounded and rushed to the nearest hospital. We don't know the status of her condition, but she was still alive when she was admitted to the hospital."

"Aw, fuck! Fuck! Hell nah ! Nah, not Epee!" Jay Wright punched his fist through the wooden door.

His wife awakened from her sound sleep when she heard his loud outbursts. She threw on her robe and came running down the stairs. Hearing her husband yell out like that could only mean that something terrible had happened.

"Baby, what is it? What's wrong? Oh my God, baby, what happened?" she questioned with fear. Jay's face said it all. She knew something was terribly wrong, and her gut instincts told her it was Epiphany. She started to cry.

"Where is she, Jay? What happened to Epee? Jay, answer me. Please say she's all right!" she demanded frantically.

"Baby, listen. We gotta go to the hospital. Epee's been hurt," he said, grabbing her close and trying to comfort her. He knew any second she was about to lose it.

"No, no, no, not my child. Where is she, Jay? What happened? What fucking hospital, huh?" she cried out and tussled to break from his arm lock.

"Stop it, Tiara. You gotta calm down. She's been shot. Now, either you gon' sit here and go crazy, or go get your shit so we can go see about her," he said, putting the situation in a better perspective.

The police offered to take them to the hospital, but Jay refused. Before he could slam the door shut, the officer handed him his card and informed him that he might have to answer some questions later. They wanted to know if he had any idea who might have wanted to harm his daughter or the young man that was with her.

"Yo, l don't know nothing right now, but whoever did this better hope you guys find 'em before I do. Now, will that be all?" Jay said, fuming.

"Mr. Wright, I know you're upset, but trust that we'll do the best that we can to find the shooter or shooters. I can only imagine how you must be feeling, because if that was my little girl lying up in some hospital bed with a gunshot wound to the chest, badly beaten, and barely holding on, I'd want to take matters into my own hands too. But you take it easy, you hear?" said the Uncle Tom Officer Johnson.

Both police officers turned to walk away. Once they reached the squad car, Riley looked at his partner with a devilish smirk on his face.

"Hey, Johnson, what was that about? You damn near told the man to take the law into his own hands."

"That's exactly what I did. I could tell you some stories about that man. Mr. J. 'Smooth Criminal' Wright, a.k.a. The Untouchable. He was big-time some years ago. The state and the Feds had him under investigation for years, but we could never get any hard evidence on that nigger to arrest or convict him, not even a petty crime. He knew the game too well. So, I was just giving the brother a little rope to hang himself with, if you know what I mean. A little encouragement never hurt nobody. Besides, knowing that scum like him is behind bars would help a lot of us sleep better at night." He laughed.

"Maybe what happened to his daughter was someone settling the score against him," said Riley.

"Yeah, could be, unless the apple doesn't fall far from the tree and she got herself caught up in her own mess. We'll just sit on this one, push it to the side, and let the animals do what they do best—kill each other off," said Smith.

Jay Wright wasted no time getting to the hospital, doing a 110 miles per hour on the Van Wyck Expressway. Under any other circumstances, Epiphany's mom would have been car sick from that type of speed, but this time was different.

"Hurry, Jay, hurry!" she hollered.

They arrived at the hospital in five minutes flat. Jay pulled up to the front of the emergency entrance. Both of them hopped out of car and rushed through the double-door entrance of the emergency waiting room.

"Sir, excuse me. You can't park there," said the flash-light security guard.

Jay pushed past the guard. Right now, his only concern was his daughter and finding out her condition. Then, he wanted the bastards responsible for trying to kill her, even if he had to take shit back to the old-school way of handling beef.

"Excuse me, miss. We're looking for our daughter, Epiphany Wright. She was shot and brought in by an ambulance a couple of hours ago. Can you tell me where we can find her, please?" Tiara said to the lady behind the information desk.

The lady punched Epiphany's name into the keyboard and directed them to the Intensive Care Unit. Once they reached the ICU, they still had to follow the same procedure again.

"Excuse me, I was told that we could find our daughter here. Her name is Epiphany Wright. She's twenty-two years old, and she was shot," said her father, this time getting even more impatient and hoping that she could assist them. Before the nurse could answer any questions, the doctor walked up.

"Excuse me. I'm Doctor Frye. Did I overhear you asking about a young woman that was shot? Are you her parents?"

"Yes, we are. Is she okay, doctor?" Tiara asked.

"Come with me, please," the doctor said. "It's been a long morning." Doctor Frye let out a sigh as the three of them began walking down the corridor. "Your daughter was shot with a .38, which is a very powerful gun, in the chest. When she was brought in, she had already lost an enormous amount of blood. We had to rush her into surgery right away. Her heart rate was fading fast, and we were without a doubt going to lose her. I had no choice, but to authorize an emergency transfusion to get her heart to start pumping again. It was successful. She also has a ruptured lung that I was able to save. That is the good news. The bad news is the baby your daughter was carrying did not make it.

"Baby! Wait a minute. What baby?" Her mother was shocked.

"Yes, your daughter was in the very, very early stage of her first trimester. Unfortunately, she lost a lot blood, so the oxygen supply to the baby was cut off. Your daughter apparently miscarried before she even got to the hospital."

Tiara's jaw dropped. Jay Wright wrapped his arm around his wife, but couldn't bear to look at her. "Also, I noticed a lot of bruises on her body, which leads me to believe that whoever shot her had beaten her first. That could've been the initial cause of the miscarriage. Either way, the child would not have survived.

"As of now, your daughter's condition is still critical. She's in a coma, and due to her injuries, she's on a respirator. Your daughter is definitely a fighter, and I strongly believe she will pull through this."

CHAPTER FOUR

On his way to the hotel he'd been staying at for the past week or so, Tucker tried calling Malikai's cell phone several times, but he didn't get an answer. He figured Malikai probably got caught up with Epiphany all over again. Even though Mali never told him, Tucker knew his boy was still sprung the fuck out over her conceited-ass.

Right now, he could've used some of his boy's advice. Malikai had been there for him from day one; before the money, cars, and even Keisha, so his feedback about what Tucker should do about the situation with Keisha, the videotape, and the nigga she was fucking on it, was needed. There was no doubt that he still loved Keisha with all his heart, but at that moment, he wished her dead. Mali would understand and never sugarcoat anything just to spare his best friend's feelings. He would give it to him raw and be honest about it.

Once he got to his room, he plopped down on the bed and stared at the ceiling until he finally fell asleep. At about six in the morning, Tucker's cell phone and two-way started going off like crazy. He ignored the first few rings, assuming it was Keisha ready to plead her case, but after tossing and turning to the vibrating sound of his two-way and the constant ringing of his cell, he became annoyed and finally went to answer his phone. The caller ID said MOMMA D.

Maybe the nigga stayed at his mother's house last night, he thought as he picked up the cell. He heard the unbearable sounds of a mother's cry. His heart ached instantly. Afraid of the possibilities, he hesitated for a moment.

"Momma D, what is it? What's wrong?"

"Oh lawd, lawd, lawd. My son is gone! He's dead, Tucker. Malikai is dead. The police came and wanted me to go identify his body, but I just can't. Tucker, what I'ma do now? My only boy is gone. What I'ma do?" she asked.

Tucker was crushed. *This can't be,* he thought. There was nothing he could say or do that would ease Mrs. McKenzie's pain.

"Momma D, get dressed. I'm on my way to get you," was all he said before ending the call.

In disbelief, he called Mali's cell repeatedly and got the voice mail each time, just like he did when he tried to reach him the night before.

"Nah, Mali, not you, dawg," Tucker mumbled.

Malikai wasn't only a business partner to Tucker; he was like his own flesh and blood—the only nigga he could trust with his life, money, girl, and his kid. Mali trusted him just the same. He was a genuine dude. Tucker knew this for a fact, because he'd tested his loyalty on several occasions, and Malikai passed every time with flying colors.

He was alone in this world for real now. He got up out of the hotel bed, got dressed, and headed over to Momma D's house.

She opened the door wearing a wrinkled dress and mismatched shoes, and her wig was on crooked. She was an emotional wreck. Tucker didn't know what else to do besides wrap his arms tightly around Momma D to console her.

"Momma D, come on. We gotta go do this. Maybe it ain't him," Tucker said, trying to be hopeful for the both of them.

"No, Tucker, I . . . I can't go see my son lying dead on some cold metal table with his brains all over the place. I just can't and I won't. The police already showed me his picture anyway. I know it's him. The streets done took my son from me. This cruel world done killed him. All I had left is gone. I just buried my husband two years ago, and now I gotta bury my son. No, you go for me, Tucker. You were like a brother to him, and I can't see my boy looking like that. I just can't."

Mrs. Delores had always been like a mother to Tucker, especially ever since his moms passed away when he was eleven. She never treated him as anything less than a son, and he depended on her for the motherly love she gave to him. She was such a sweet old lady, the type that would feed you a good hot meal if you were hungry and give you half of her last dollar if you needed it. Tucker had mad love and respect for her. He even gave her the nicknames Momma D and Mom Dukes, both short for Delores, her first name. So, to see her suffering caused Tucker a great deal of pain.

He planted a kiss on her forehead and headed for the morgue. On his way there, it was so ironic that Puffy's tribute to Biggie, "I'll Be Missing You," was playing on the radio. Tucker refused to believe it until he saw him.

He phoned his boys from the Dirty South, Peewee and Cornell, to tell them the news.

Everything became a reality when he stepped into the morgue. Tucker's body caught an instant chill from the cool temperature in the place, and the smell of dead people gave him a nauseating feeling. The coroner asked him what his relationship was to the deceased.

"I'm his brother."

Tucker followed the man to another room, where he saw his best friend lying dead with a head the size of a basketball and his brains oozing out on the table. His stomach felt very weak from the sight of Malikai, and his emotions were mixed with pain, anger, and sorrow. Mali was the closest thing to a brother he had, and his loss was too great to ignore.

Tucker disregarded the words of his father and shed a few tears. Then he started to beat up on himself, feeling responsible for not being there to protect Malikai. He failed as his brother's keeper. To him, he was just as much to blame as the nigga that pulled the trigger.

Looking at Malikai lying there like that was hard on his eyes. Tucker leaned over Mali's corpse and thought about all the good times they shared. There were so many memories to hold on to. Malikai, twenty-five, was too young to die. He was just starting to live life, and just like that, it was over.

"Damn, Mali, we should have left this drug game alone along time ago. It's over for me now. This shit is so played out. I'm done! I don't want to do this shit no more," Tucker spoke to Malikai as if he could hear him.

The shine was no longer worth the headache, heartache, or losses that come along with the territory.

Tucker was eighteen when he started selling drugs, and it took him every bit of the ten years he spent hustling to realize that this game wasn't fair. It was a lot of money to be made, but it would never make you rich, nor would it let you go without paying a price. Either you lost yourself, your freedom, or your soul at the end of either road, and it wasn't worth it. Tucker would never gain anything from hustling that could replace his loss, so for him this was the end of the road. Malikai's death was surely his wake-up call, while he still had half a soul left. The game, as he knew it, was over.

ORDER FORM
URBAN BOOKS, LLC
97 N. 18th Street
Wyandanch, NY 11798

Name: (please print):_____

Address: _____

City/State: _____

Zip: _____

QTY	TITLES	PRICE
	16 On The Block	$14.95
	A Girl From Flint	$14.95
	A Pimp's Life	$14.95
	Baltimore Chronicles	$14.95
	Baltimore Chronicles 2	$14.95
	Betrayal	$14.95
	Black Diamond	$14.95
	Black Diamond 2	$14.95
	Black Friday	$14.95
	Both Sides Of The Fence	$14.95
	Both Sides Of The Fence 2	$14.95
	California Connection	$14.95

Shipping and handling-add $3.50 for 1st book, then $1.75 for each additional book.
Please send a check payable to:
Urban Books, LLC
Please allow 4–6 weeks for delivery

ORDER FORM
URBAN BOOKS, LLC
97 N. 18th Street
Wyandanch, NY 11798

Name (please print):_____

Address: _____

City/State: _____

Zip: _____

QTY	TITLES	PRICE
	California Connection 2	$14.95
	Cheesecake And Teardrops	$14.95
	Congratulations	$14.95
	Crazy In Love	$14.95
	Cyber Case	$14.95
	Denim Diaries	$14.95
	Diary Of A Mad First Lady	$14.95
	Diary Of A Stalker	$14.95
	Diary Of A Street Diva	$14.95
	Diary Of A Young Girl	$14.95
	Dirty Money	$14.95
	Dirty To The Grave	$14.95

Shipping and handling-add $3.50 for 1st book, then $1.75 for each additional book.
Please send a check payable to:
Urban Books, LLC
Please allow 4-6 weeks for delivery

ORDER FORM
URBAN BOOKS, LLC
97 N. 18th Street
Wyandanch, NY 11798

Name (please print):_____

Address: _____

City/State: _____

Zip: _____

QTY	TITLES	PRICE
	Gunz And Roses	$14.95
	Happily Ever Now	$14.95
	Hell Has No Fury	$14.95
	Hush	$14.95
	If It Isn't love	$14.95
	Kiss Kiss Bang Bang	$14.95
	Last Breath	$14.95
	Little Black Girl Lost	$14.95
	Little Black Girl Lost 2	$14.95
	Little Black Girl Lost 3	$14.95
	Little Black Girl Lost 4	$14.95
	Little Black Girl Lost 5	$14.95

Shipping and handling-add $3.50 for 1st book, then $1.75 for each additional book.
Please send a check payable to:
    Urban Books, LLC
Please allow 4-6 weeks for delivery

ORDER FORM
URBAN BOOKS, LLC
97 N. 18th Street
Wyandanch, NY 11798

Name (please print):_____

Address: _____

City/State: _____

Zip: _____

QTY	TITLES	PRICE
	Loving Dasia	$14.95
	Material Girl	$14.95
	Moth To A Flame	$14.95
	Mr. High Maintenance	$14.95
	My Little Secret	$14.95
	Naughty	$14.95
	Naughty 2	$14.95
	Naughty 3	$14.95
	Queen Bee	$14.95
	Say It Ain't So	$14.95
	Snapped	$14.95
	Snow White	$14.95

Shipping and handling-add $3.50 for 1st book, then $1.75 for each additional book.
Please send a check payable to:
    Urban Books, LLC
Please allow 4-6 weeks for delivery

ORDER FORM
URBAN BOOKS, LLC
97 N. 18th Street
Wyandanch, NY 11798

Name (please print):_____

Address: _____

City/State: _____

Zip: _____

QTY	TITLES	PRICE
	Spoil Rotten	$14.95
	Supreme Clientele	$14.95
	The Cartel	$14.95
	The Cartel 2	$14.95
	The Cartel 3	$14.95
	The Dopefiend	$14.95
	The Dopeman Wife	$14.95
	The Prada Plan	$14.95
	The Prada Plan 2	$14.95
	Where There Is Smoke	$14.95
	Where There Is Smoke 2	$14.95

Shipping and handling-add $3.50 for 1st book, then $1.75 for each additional book.
Please send a check payable to:
Urban Books, LLC
Please allow 4–6 weeks for delivery

ORDER FORM
URBAN BOOKS, LLC
97 N. 18th Street
Wyandanch, NY 11798

Name (please print):_____

Address: _____

City/State: _____

Zip: _____

QTY	TITLES	PRICE

Shipping and handling-add $3.50 for 1st book, then $1.75 for each additional book.
Please send a check payable to:
Urban Books, LLC
Please allow 4-6 weeks for delivery

ORDER FORM
URBAN BOOKS, LLC
97 N. 18th Street
Wyandanch, NY 11798

Name (please print):_____

Address: _____

City/State: _____

Zip: _____

QTY	TITLES	PRICE

Shipping and handling-add \$3.50 for 1st book, then \$1.75 for each additional book.

Please send a check payable to:
        Urban Books, LLC
Please allow 4–6 weeks for delivery